DOCTOR WHO

THE FIRES OF POMPEII

DOCTOR WHO

THE FIRES
OF POMPEII

Based on the BBC television adventure
The Fires of Pompeii by James Moran

JAMES MORAN

BBC Books, an imprint of Ebury Publishing
20 Vauxhall Bridge Road,
London SW1V 2SA

BBC Books is part of the Penguin Random House group of companies
whose addresses can be found at global.penguinrandomhouse.com

Penguin
Random House
UK

First published by BBC Books in 2022

www.penguin.co.uk

A CIP catalogue record for this book is available from the British Library

ISBN 9781785947797

Editorial director: Albert DePetrillo
Project editor: Steve Cole
Cover design: Two Associates
Cover illustration: Anthony Dry

Printed and bound in Great Britain by Clays Ltd, Elcograf S.p.A.

The authorised representative in the EEA is Penguin Random House Ireland,
Morrison Chambers, 32 Nassau Street, Dublin D02 YH68

Penguin Random House is committed to a sustainable future
for our business, our readers and our planet. This book is made
from Forest Stewardship Council® certified paper.

Contents

For Gracie.
Hurry up and get old enough to read this.
But also, stay a kid forever. I did,
and can highly recommend it.

For my mum, who always despaired of me reading
'rubbish', but somehow convinced the library to
let me have a full adult card when I was 8 so
I could read even more of it.

And for you, whoever you are, reading this.
You can be anyone you want. Just be someone kind.

Prologue

Dramatis personae

They had slept, for thousands of years, deep under the ground, unaware that they were even still alive.

No dreams troubled their slumber. A sleep so deep, it may as well have been death. They were the last of their kind, fleeing from a lost planet, searching for a new home. They hadn't intended to come to this world; the conditions were all wrong for them. Too cold, too wet, too small. A tiny, dirty ball of mud, infested with unremarkable, watery, cattle-like creatures. They hadn't even given the place a second look, dismissing it immediately. There would be better worlds, worthier homes, more comfortable temperatures.

But things didn't work out the way they'd planned. Sloppy navigation and a series of malfunctions resulted in them getting pulled down by the mud planet, and they fell, so fast, so hard, it was almost over before they knew it.

They knew they couldn't survive this. With mere seconds to go before impact, they contemplated the end.

If this was to be the final line of their story, then they were still proud to tell it. Proud of who they were, who they had been, the mighty world they had once ruled.

Their main regret was that nobody would ever know who they used to be. They would be forgotten, for ever. They deserved better than this. They deserved an empire. But they would face their end with honour and stoicism.

They hit the ground, everything went dark, and that seemed to be the end of it.

Thousands of years later, the earth shook violently, disturbing their rest. They were surprised to find that their consciousness had survived, as had their physical bodies, albeit fragmented into dust. But it was enough. Enough to be aware of their surroundings, aware that they were still very much alive. Their story was not yet over. A new chapter had begun.

Bodies could be rebuilt, gradually. Their ship was mostly gone, although part of it survived, and could be repurposed. But they would need help.

Their minds reached out, to see what was nearby.

Examining the watery, cattle-like creatures more closely, they were thrilled to discover that they could reach into their minds, and whisper to them. And whisper they did. They found the watery creatures to be slow-witted and limited in scope, knowing nothing of the stars. But they were able to fill those tiny minds with information, commands, instructions. Their words fitted neatly alongside the watery cattle's superstition and willingness to serve. They had long searched for a new planet to rule, and the natives here were ready for gods to rule over them. It was almost a shame that the servile cattle would eventually have to be destroyed, when they had served their purpose. A necessary sacrifice, to further the cause.

It was going to take a while. But they had already waited for a long, long time and could wait some more. They were nothing if not patient.

Patient, and ruthless.

Chapter I

Veni, vidi, vici

Donna Noble was worried. This was her first proper journey with the person she knew as the Doctor, so her concern was understandable. But even that description was wrong, for starters. That was the thing – he wasn't a person, was he?

He certainly looked like one. Although they were inside the TARDIS, an alien ship that travelled through space and time, and he was operating switches and levers that looked impossible to decipher, he looked fairly normal. Too many teeth, of course. And his knees were far too knobbly, and his hair seemed to get higher and higher every day; she had no idea what sort of weird space gel he was using on it. But he still looked like he could be human. Even though he definitely wasn't.

Before Donna had met him, she had lived a normal life on Earth. She'd had no idea that life existed on other planets. But then she'd been caught up in a plot by her fiancé to feed her to some alien spider babies – as you do – and suddenly the Doctor had come crashing into her life to save the day. He'd offered to take her with him after that, to travel through the universe and see the sights, but it was all a bit too much for her at the time. Discovering the man who had asked you to marry him was faking it, and that aliens were real, *and* that you were about to become spider lunch, all on the same day? No thanks. That was more than enough excitement. It was too new, too dangerous, too scary. So she had turned him down.

As soon as he left and she went back to her normal daily routine, she realised what a huge mistake she had made. Ever since then, for months, she'd been trying to find him again. Investigating anything that might have alien involvement – conspiracies, anything weird, she was on it like a car bonnet. She knew that if she found another secret alien plot, he would probably turn up to get involved, and she was going to make sure she was there when he did. She almost missed him; it was a close thing that hinged on the tiniest moment. If she'd turned right instead of left that day, who knows what might have happened, or not happened.

Now, however, she'd finally found him again, and her wish had been granted. She was travelling with him, off on an adventure. Nothing to worry about. Nothing at all. Dream come true, all that jazz, blah, blah, blah.

Still, though.

Her mind raced through several levels of anxiety without stopping. She knew that he wasn't a person, he'd told her that already. He was some sort of alien spaceman. Or should she say spaceperson? Or maybe it was something totally different. They might be called 'blorgs' or 'farnkangles' or something – what if she'd already offended him? Then again, some aliens were animals, not people, maybe he was one of those. Spacecreature? Oh blimey, what if he was a giant insect or something, or like the aliens in *V*, that old TV show; what if his 'skin' was just rubber and when he was relaxing he pulled it off to reveal a big lizard face? What if he ate gerbils? Her mate Caz had a gerbil. Donna had always thought it was a horrible little weird thing, but she wouldn't want anyone to eat it, especially not in front of her. Maybe he didn't even eat gerbils. Maybe it was worse. Maybe he ate humans! Maybe that's why he had been so keen to bring her along. Maybe when she started wandering around the TARDIS she'd find a big larder full of people ... No, that was silly. She was being silly. He was nice.

Wasn't he?

Back when she'd initially turned him down, she'd told him to find someone to travel with. She felt he'd come down a bit hard on the alien threat at the time, much harder than necessary, and she knew that he would need reining in now and again. It was another reason she'd decided against going with him. She didn't want to be the one in the position of arguing with an incredibly powerful alien.

But now she was here, they seemed to be getting along really well. They had a proper, friendly relationship. She knew he'd listen to her, and respect her opinions. She'd spent so long trying to track him down, so why was she suddenly having second thoughts? This was everything she'd been dreaming of, for months. He'd saved her life, after all, so he must be nice. Yeah. That sounded plausible.

Her anxiety rerouted itself down another brain pathway, as anxiety does, and found something else to worry about. Maybe *he* was perfectly safe, but maybe the journey itself would kill her. She'd only had Earth-bound escapades with him, but now they were off somewhere else, some*when* else, could be anywhere in time or space. What if they landed on a planet with giant insects? Or gerbil-eating lizards? Or human-eating giant gerbils? What was she thinking? She had just walked into his SPACESHIP, and now they were in SPACE, travelling through TIME, and he was looking at her FACE and saying her NAME—

'Donna!' the Doctor shouted, finally, clapping his hands. 'Snap out of it! Are you all right?'

Donna jumped, startled, going on the defensive. 'Yeah? Yeah! Course I'm all right, why wouldn't I be all right, are you saying I'm not all right, maybe *you're* not all right, ever think about that?'

'Sorry. It's just that you stopped talking for several minutes. I thought you might have died.'

'Ohhhhh, now he's a comedian.'

The Doctor smiled at her, not unkindly. 'It can be a bit overwhelming,' he said. 'I forget that, sometimes. Should have eased you into it.'

Donna bluffed, quickly. 'What do you mean? I'm not scared, alien planets don't bother me, you should see my local on speed-date night during happy hour, it's absolute carnage, nothing scares me, mate.'

'I didn't say scared,' said the Doctor.

'Good, doesn't matter, because I'm not scared anyway.'

The Doctor seemed to think about it for a moment. He clicked his fingers, smiling. 'Tell you what. Let's do it in stages. Earth first, then other planets.'

Donna pouted. 'Oh, we've already done Earth, I'm bored of Earth. If I wanted Earth, I'd have stayed at home, I didn't need to come in here and listen to your lip just to hang around Earth.'

'Don't worry. It's our first proper journey together. It'll be good, I promise. I'll make sure. Trust me, I'm a doctor. Literally. Well, not literally, but you know what I mean.'

The Doctor ran around the console, wildly throwing levers and hitting buttons, seemingly at random, showing off. The TARDIS juddered, and lurched to one side.

Donna frowned at him. The other anxiety-inducing possibility, of course, was that he had absolutely no idea what he was doing, and would crash them into a star before they even got anywhere.

'I don't mean to be rude,' she said, a statement which usually preceded her being rude, 'but can you actually fly this thing, or are you just some sort of space lunatic?'

The Doctor scoffed, as if it was the most ridiculous question he'd ever heard, which Donna doubted was anywhere near the truth. 'Donna, I'm a Time Lord, there is literally nobody in the universe more qualified to fly this thi- this TARDIS. You're in safe hands. Now, watch and learn.'

He gave her what she supposed was meant to be a reassuring look, and pulled at a lever, which promptly snapped off in his hand. He spun the broken lever around and pocketed it, trying to style it out.

'Ah,' he said. 'Keep meaning to get that fixed . . .'

'If you get us killed before we even land, I will kill you.'

'Everything's under control. We're landing! Get ready! *Abeamus!*'

'What's *a bay-a-moose* when it's at home?'

'It's Latin for *allons-y.*'

The Doctor threw one final switch and bounded over to the doors.

'Why are you saying it in Latin?' Donna demanded, hurrying after him. 'What possible reason—'

*

They stepped outside, into the hustle and bustle of a busy market. Not just any busy market. A busy market back in Earth's distant past.

'Ancient Rome!' beamed the Doctor, looking pretty pleased with himself. 'Well, it's not ancient to *them*, of course,' he clarified. 'To all intents and purposes, right now, this is brand new Rome!'

Donna slowed to a stop as she looked all around. It was a lot to take in. The stallholders selling their wares, people bargaining, the clothing, amphorae, crates of chickens, the genuine old buildings – but not just old buildings, these were shiny and new buildings, because this was the present day to the locals, as the Doctor had pointed out.

She struggled to find the words. The scale of it hit her. She had travelled through time, to ancient Rome. She couldn't quite get her head around it.

'This . . . this is not today,' she managed to say.

'Course it's today! Every day is today, as long as it's today. Basic time theory, that. Otherwise things would get far too confusing. Even more confusing, I mean. Look at all this!'

The Doctor strode forward, exploring, drinking in the sights, sounds and smells.

'Ah, it never gets old,' he said, delighted. 'This, I mean, travelling through time and space. Every time I land, it's always exciting to see what's out there, meet new people, try different food. Usually some risk of danger everywhere, sure, but if you approach each new trip with a positive mindset then you'll always be pleasantly surprised, that's what I say.'

Donna was just staring at everything, silently.

'Got to jump in with both feet,' continued the Doctor. 'Even if you do sometimes end up eating something that makes you feel a bit iffy. Depending on the planet, of course, sometimes your food disagrees with you, sometimes you disagree with the food, sometimes you *are* the food. Safe enough on Earth, though, not much risk of being eaten. As long as you avoid certain times and places. You can't make friends with dinosaurs. Believe me, I've tried. You all right there? You've gone all quiet again. You sure you're not ill?'

Donna was still attempting to find the right words in the right order. 'No, I mean . . . it's not *today*-today,' she said. 'It's before? Before today? Not the present day. The past! It's the past. We're actually in the past. Are we? Are we really here or just watching? Can they even see and hear us?'

A market trader held out a gourd to Donna. 'Gourd, madam? Very reasonable.'

Donna stared at him. 'No, thanks, I . . . I've already got one. Doctor!'

She followed him round a corner, struggling to keep up. This part of the market was filled with interesting fruits and spices. It smelled amazing.

Donna tried again. 'We're in the past!'

'Exactly! First trip, it's got to be a bit special. You don't want to see the boring old present, do you? Thought you'd fancy having a look at what it was really like, back in the past. Soak up all that past-y goodness. Ooh, past-y, pasty, now I'm getting hungry. Is that a mango? Have they discovered mangos yet? I'm craving a mango.'

Donna touched a wall, running her fingers over the texture. She picked up a cup, and stared at it. Normally, in her everyday life, this cup would be in a museum, or dug up out of the ground, ancient, faded and cracked. But right here, right now, the cup had only just been made, the metal bright and shiny, with a beautiful design all around the outside. It wasn't an antique, it was a normal household object, for real live people to drink from as they laughed and sang songs. Without warning, tears welled up in her eyes. She wasn't expecting to be moved by something so simple.

'Oh my god,' she said. 'It's so . . . it's so Roman! Doctor, this is brilliant, I don't even know what to say.'

'That's got to be a first.'

The Doctor yelped as Donna impulsively grabbed him in a bear hug, and squeezed him tightly. 'Thank you,' she whispered, quickly wiping away a tear. This meant a lot to her; she hadn't realised quite how much. She felt unexpectedly connected to the past, now that she could see it. It was a reminder that her home had a rich history, all of it worth remembering, good and bad.

'All part of the service. Now if you could let go, I can't actually breathe,' gasped the Doctor.

'Yeah, sorry.' Donna released him from her grip.

'Where to now?' said the Doctor, eyeing up the various stalls. 'Ooh! I wonder if they've got any togas? I always quite fancied a toga.'

'You, in a toga? It'd be like a cape on a broomstick. A sail wrapped around a ship's mast. A big top circus tent that's come loose at the bottom. Just flapping about in the wind. Nobody wants to see that.'

'I bet I could carry it off.'

'That's what worries me,' said Donna. 'But I still can't believe this. I'm here, in Rome. Donna Noble is in Rome! This is so weird. I mean . . . everyone here is dead.'

She stared at the people walking around. Every one of them was long gone in her present, but right now, here they all were, alive and kicking. It was a bit of a strange feeling.

'Well, I wouldn't go telling them that,' said the Doctor.

'You know what I mean,' said Donna. 'This is the past so, back home, they've been dead for thousands of years.'

'Who says your present is the actual present?'

Donna scrunched up her face. 'What do you mean, the actual present?'

'Suppose I'd taken you to the future. People there

think they're in the actual present. What if they looked at you and went, "Ooh, look at her, she's been dead for thousands of years!"'

'No, but that wouldn't be true, would it? I'm still alive.'

'Not to them. To them, they're in the present, and *you're* from the past.'

Donna shivered a little bit. 'So, which present is the real present?'

'There isn't one! It's all relative, isn't it? Time is an illusion. Lunchtime doubly so, as a wise man once said. I miss him a lot, must pop back and see him again. Speaking of lunch, I'm starving.'

'You don't make a lot of sense, do you?'

'Nah, can't be bothered.'

Donna stopped as a thought struck her. 'Hold on, hold on. I spoke to that man, the one with the gourd. And he spoke to me.'

'Yeah?'

Donna marched over to another market trader. 'You! Hello! Can you understand me?'

The trader looked at her quizzically. 'Course I can.'

'That's the TARDIS. Translation circuits,' said the Doctor distantly, looking all about. 'Where *is* everything? I used to know this place like the back of my hand. Mind you, that was several different hands ago.'

Donna stared at a hand-painted stall sign, suspiciously. The sign read *Two amphorae for the price of one*.

English. How did that work? Were they *really* in the past? Donna looked around, and saw several more signs in English. That couldn't be right. If this had all been some big trick, she was about to get very angry. And when Donna Noble got angry, things got broken.

'Hold on a minute,' she said, pointing at the stall. 'That sign's in English. Are you having me on? Are we in Epcot?'

'Nope, TARDIS translation circuits again. Gets inside your head, just makes it look like English. Works both ways, affects what you say, too. They don't just hear the Latin after you've said it in English, you're actually speaking it right now.'

'Seriously? I just said "seriously" in Latin?'

'Yep!'

Donna smiled from ear to ear, delighted. 'That's amazing! Look at me, swanning around ancient Rome, talking Latin, giving it the old *I, Clavdivs*!'

The Doctor looked totally lost. 'I Clav . . . what . . . ?'

'It's what we called *I, Claudius* on telly, the "u"s looked like "v"s, so we always said "I, Clavdivs" for a laugh. It was hilarious!'

The Doctor wasn't laughing. 'OK . . .'

'You had to be there, really. Hold on! What if I said something in actual Latin? How would that come out? Like "veni, vidi, vici", my dad says that when he comes back from the football. If I said "veni, vidi, vici" to that lot, what would it sound like to them?'

The Doctor frowned. 'You always have to think of difficult questions, don't you?'

'I'm gonna try it!' Donna walked up to a cheerful stallholder, who was selling a variety of wares. She smiled at him, and he beamed back.

'Afternoon sweetheart, what can I get you, my love?'

Donna cleared her throat, and announced, '*Veni, vidi, vici!*'

She stood there, waiting for him to be impressed. Instead, the stallholder looked at her, sympathetically, as if she was a child. He replied to her loudly and slowly, in the time-honoured fashion of people who didn't speak a foreign language, but thought that increasing the volume and decreasing the speed would suffice. 'Sorry! Me no speak Celtic! No can do, missy.'

Donna looked embarrassed, and slowly shuffled back to the Doctor, who had watched the whole exchange with amusement. 'How's he mean, Celtic?' she asked.

'Welsh,' said the Doctor, surprised. 'You sound Welsh. There we are, I've learnt something.'

'Why did he have a Cockney accent? What's that all about?'

'Every region has different accents, dialects. TAR-DIS translation circuits allow for that, and turn it into something you're familiar with. He's clearly a hard-working street trader, from a working-class region of

17

Rome; Cockney was the closest approximation that would make sense to you, so that's what you heard.'

The more the Doctor explained it, the more Donna wanted to pick it apart. 'So . . . what if someone has a Cockney accent already, but speaks Welsh, to another Cockney?'

'I . . . OK, I really don't know.' The Doctor's frown was immense. 'Is that the most important thing you want to find out right now? We're in ancient Rome!'

Donna couldn't help feeling slightly disappointed. 'Honestly, sometimes it feels like you just go stomping around the place without even knowing how half of this stuff works.'

'I mean, if we're splitting hairs, then yes, fair enough.'

They walked off down a side street, still talking animatedly, oblivious to the fact that they were being followed. A young woman lurked in the shadows, watching them, glancing back at the TARDIS. She wore burgundy robes, her face was painted white, and there were strange patterns etched onto her skin.

Her name was Mira. She was a Soothsayer. And she had been expecting them.

Donna was still enjoying the sights and sounds of this strange new world. Only it wasn't a new world, it was her own world, her planet. She remembered an old saying from somewhere, the future is the undiscovered country. What would that would make the past? Forgotten country? Something like that.

Hold on, thought Donna. *Our outfits!* Donna was suddenly very aware that their clothes were from another era. What if people realised they were from the future? Weren't there rules about keeping a low profile? Don't step on a butterfly, and all that? Not that she would, not deliberately of course. Great, now she was worried about accidentally squashing butterflies, too.

'Doctor! Don't our clothes look a bit weird?' she asked, watching where she stepped, checking obsessively for any random butterflies. 'We must look weird to them.'

'Nah,' breezed the Doctor. 'Ancient Rome, anything goes. It's like Soho. But bigger. And not quite as many phone shops.'

'Oh, right. Have you been here before, then?'

'Ages ago,' said the Doctor, suddenly looking a bit guilty about something. 'And before you ask, that fire had nothing to do with me. Well, not very much. Well, a little bit. Well . . . But I never got the chance to look around properly! The Colosseum! The Pantheon! The Circus Maximus! Although, you'd expect them to be looming by now, where is everything? I admit, it's been a while, but you can't really avoid them, they're huge. Let's try down this way.'

The Doctor and Donna walked off down another

street, followed by the Soothsayer, who was careful to stay hidden. They turned a corner, and stopped abruptly when they saw it. They couldn't miss it, really. An enormous mountain, in the distance. Wisps of smoke dancing about the summit.

It looked awfully familiar.

They both had that uncomfortable twinge in their stomachs that something was terribly, terribly wrong here.

'I'm not an expert,' said Donna. 'But aren't there supposed to be Seven Hills of Rome? How come they've only got one?'

Abruptly, with a low rumble, the ground started to shake. And then everything else did. Walls. Buildings. Stalls. People quickly ran for cover, into doorways, under awnings, but nobody seemed scared – quite the opposite. They weren't even surprised, they'd obviously experienced this before, several times. Many were even smiling, rolling their eyes, as if it was nothing more than a mild inconvenience.

They weren't at all worried, because they didn't know what it meant.

But the Doctor and Donna did, even though they really didn't want to.

More smoke belched out the top of the mountain, and the ground shook even more violently.

It was Mount Vesuvius.

An active volcano, almost ready to erupt.

This wasn't Rome.

'Hold up a minute,' said Donna. 'One mountain. With smoke. Which makes this . . .'

'Pompeii,' said the Doctor. 'We're in Pompeii. And it's Volcano Day . . .'

Chapter II

In media res

Out on the streets of Pompeii, the earthquake faded and stopped, as things gradually got back to normal. The Doctor and Donna stared all around them, poised for action in case it started again. Strangely, though, everybody still looked perfectly happy, as if nothing was out of the ordinary. They were clearly used to this; most of them even found it funny. But the new arrivals didn't find it amusing at all.

Donna had learned about Pompeii at school. In AD 79, everyone in the city was killed when Vesuvius erupted, burying the town in ash and rocks. Nobody even knew the word 'volcano'; they knew that sometimes fire came out of the mountain, but had no idea it was causing the earthquakes or could be so powerfully destructive, so it caught them all by surprise. The loss of life was enormous. It was one of history's greatest catastrophes, and Donna and the Doctor would be right in the middle of it, unless they got out of there immediately.

A friendly market trader smiled at their shocked faces. 'You must be new here,' he said. 'Don't worry, it's always doing that. They say Vulcan's in there, he must be angry today. Should be fine now. His bark's worse than his bite. He has a bit of a rumble, breathes out some smoke, shakes everything around for a bit, then he calms down again. Nothing to be scared of.'

The Doctor nodded. 'Right. Vulcan. The god of fire. Which would make that Vesuvius, I suppose.'

'Right you are, chief.'

Donna leaned over to the Doctor, and tried to mutter as quietly as possible. 'Vesuvius, as in, the great big volcano? The one that buried Pompeii? This Pompeii, the Pompeii we're standing in right now?'

'Yep,' said the Doctor.

'And it's gonna—'

'Sure is.'

'Which means—'

'It does.'

'So we should probably—'

'Exactly.'

'OK, then.'

'OK, then.'

They stood there, staring at Vesuvius, trying to remain calm.

Three seconds later, they were running full speed through the streets, back the way they came.

'Of all the places and times to land,' yelled Donna. 'Millions of years of history! An entire planet full of different cities! None of which are sitting slap bang next to an active volcano that's about to blow up!'

'Don't tell me,' the Doctor yelled back. 'Tell the TARDIS. Something must have pulled us off course.'

'Yeah, probably that stupid lever you never get fixed! I knew you didn't know how to fly that thing properly. How many other bits of it are broken?'

'None,' said the Doctor. 'She's in perfect working order. Well ... I mean, when you say "broken", how are you defining that, exactly?'

'How are you even alive after all these years? I suppose I should consider myself lucky you didn't land us INSIDE the volcano.'

'Stop using the v-word! Let's just get out of here!'

'Anywhere else would have done,' said Donna, exasperated. 'I'd have been happy with a winter weekend at the Rhyl Sun Centre in the Eighties, we had a school trip there when I was a kid. It was rubbish but, on balance, I can't complain because it didn't EXPLODE!'

They got back to where they'd landed, and looked all around wildly. There was no sign of the TARDIS. The Doctor looked at Donna, at a loss. 'Ah,' he said. 'Right, er ...'

Donna slowly grasped the Doctor by the lapels on his suit, and drew him close. She spoke in a low, threatening voice that was somehow even scarier than when she was shouting. 'Now, listen to me, spaceman. This is very, very important. Do not – I repeat, do *not* – tell me that the TARDIS is missing.'

'OK,' said the Doctor, looking guilty. He bit his lip nervously.

Donna waited until she'd had enough of the awkward silence. 'Well, where is it, then?'

'You told me not to tell you . . .'

'Oi! Don't get clever in Latin! Just find it, and get us out of here, before that great big mountain goes kaboom!'

'Let go of me! Hang on, the TARDIS wouldn't just vanish, somebody must have moved it. I'm sure there's a perfectly reasonable explanation.' The Doctor ran over to the cheerful, Cockney-sounding stallholder from earlier, waving at him. 'Excuse me! Hello! There was a box here, a big blue box, sort of box-shaped, just over here. Did you see where it went?'

The stallholder grinned proudly. 'Yeah! I sold it, didn't I?'

The Doctor boggled at him. 'Sold it? But . . . it wasn't yours to sell!'

'Listen mush, if it's on my patch, it's for sale. Them's the rules. Got 15 sesterces for it. Lovely jubbly!'

'Who did you sell it to?'

'Old Caecilius. Saw him coming, ha! He'll buy any old rubbish if he thinks it looks nice, he reckons he's an expert. Marble expert, yeah – anything else, clueless. Just my type of customer. Look, if you want a barney about it, go take it up with him. He's up on Foss Street, big fancy villa, can't miss it, place is dripping in marble, he loves it.'

Relief flooded the Doctor's face. 'Thank you!' He ran over to Donna, who was hyperventilating a little. 'Panic over! Bloke called Caecilius has got it, we need to find Foss Street, he's got a big marble villa. Let's split up, cover more ground. Meet back at the market in half an hour.'

'OK,' said Donna. 'Next time, just a suggestion, take it or leave it, but maybe check the space GPS or something before we step outside the doors, yeah? If it's not too much to ask. And would it kill you to put a clock up on the wall?'

They ran off, going their separate ways, each hoping they would find the TARDIS before it was too late.

Mira the Soothsayer stepped out of the shadows, watching them go.

She placed both of her palms over her eyes, revealing an elaborate drawing of an eye on the back of each hand. Her body stiffened, as she formed a psychic link with another Soothsayer named Spurrina, elsewhere in the city. The link allowed them to communicate with each other; they could see and hear both sides of the conversation even as they strode along the streets, hands over their eyes but still able to see where they were going.

People in the street gave Mira a wide berth as she whispered now, 'Strangers. They have come, as foretold in the prophecy. They have the box. The blue box.'

Spurrina responded in her mind: 'Impossible.'

'I will follow them and return to you,' said Mira. 'Find the text! You'll see!'

Mira lowered her hands, looking around for the strange travellers. They weren't too hard to keep track of, even though they had separated. They had seemed upset about something, running around, arguing, always arguing; even when they agreed on something, it still felt like an argument. Their clothing was odd, too. Mira couldn't quite put her finger on it, they just felt all wrong. They weren't simply not of Pompeii – they were not of *anywhere*. They didn't belong in this city, this world, this time. She couldn't understand how she knew that, but it was as clear as the colours in a painting. They were from very far away, not just physically, but in years, too. The way her childhood memories were from a different time, so too were these visitors, somehow. The concepts were unfamiliar to her, unsettling. How could someone be from another time, yet also be here now? It hurt her head to even think about it.

The strangers drew too far apart to follow both, so the Soothsayer stayed with the loud one. She was easier to keep track of because she kept shouting, even when she was alone, and her flame-red hair was a helpful beacon in the crowds. She went around in several circles, before ending up at the main city amphitheatre, where she marched around shouting, 'Testing, testing, one two three,' for some reason. Then she ran off, back into the streets, heading to the market again. The Soothsayer was even more confused about the strangers' purpose now.

She kept following the loud one, who went around in more circles until the tall one eventually reappeared from another street, and they ran into each other. Mira retreated into the shadows, to listen to their conversation.

'There you are,' Donna told the Doctor, relieved. 'I thought I'd lost you for a minute. Lost in Pompeii, with that thing ready to blow up any second.'

'Don't panic,' said the Doctor. 'We've got a while until it erupts.'

'Good. Why are we both running so fast, then?'

'Because I'm panicking a bit . . . Anyway, I've found Foss Street. Come on, it's up this way. We can get the TARDIS back and be on our way.'

'Perfect, I know exactly where to take it, I've found this big sort of amphitheatre thing, I think it's where Pink Floyd did that concert – or where they *will* do it, in the future, that's a bit confusing, but you know what

I mean – anyway, we can start there, gather everyone together. Ooh, maybe they've got a great big bell we could ring or something? Have they invented bells yet?'

The Doctor stopped running, confused. 'Hold on, hold on,' he said. 'Blimey, sometimes I have trouble following your train of thought, and then sometimes your train of thought just jumps the tracks and lands in the middle of next week . . . Back it up a bit. What do you want a bell for?'

'To warn everyone. Start the evacuation. What time does Vesuvius erupt? When's it due?'

'Twenty-third of August, which means it happens tomorrow.'

'Oh, plenty of time! That's a relief. We could get everyone out easy!'

'Yeah, except we're not going to,' said the Doctor.

Donna looked at him. 'But . . . that's what you do,' she said, confused. 'You're the Doctor. You save people.'

'Not this time. Pompeii is a fixed point in history. What happens, happens, there's no stopping it.'

'Says who?'

'Says me.'

'What, and you're in charge?'

They squared up to each other like boxers before a match, almost nose to nose.

The Doctor weighed up his credentials aloud. 'TARDIS, Time Lord, yeah.'

Donna threw down some credentials of her own. 'Donna, human, no!' Admittedly, her declaration didn't sound quite as impressive, but she didn't care, she wasn't having this at all. 'I don't need your permission, I'll tell them myself.'

'You stand in the market place announcing the end of the world, they'll just think you're making it up like a silly old soothsayer.' He waved some jazz hands for emphasis. 'Now, come on. TARDIS. We're getting out of here.' The Doctor walked off, without waiting for her to follow.

Donna shouted after him. 'Well I might just have something to say about that, spaceman!'

'Oh, I bet you will!' he shouted back.

Donna was just about to unleash a stream of rude words that she very much doubted there was a Latin translation for, when she was interrupted by the most unearthly, gut-wrenching sound filling the air. A long, drawn out groan, like the metal buckling on the *Titanic*, like souls lost at sea, or a broken air-raid siren.

Everyone in the street stopped what they were doing to listen. People came out of their houses, startled. This was new. Nobody laughed this time.

It was incredibly loud, the resonance making cups and teeth rattle. It didn't seem to be coming from anywhere, it felt like it was just in their heads. But it was real. The vibrating dust on the ground made that clear.

It went on and on, for almost a full minute, gradually lowering in pitch, and eventually petering out.

In the distance, there was a small puff of smoke from Vesuvius.

'What the hell was that?' said Donna.

'Must have been the mountain,' said the Doctor. 'I don't know exactly what, but it's got to be part of it. We'd better get a move on.

He ran off, and Donna followed him this time. 'I hope you've brought enough money to buy it back off this Caecilius bloke,' she said.

'We'll be fine,' said the Doctor. 'Something I can't quite get my head around, though. What did he buy a big, blue, wooden box *for*?'

Chapter III

Caecilius est in hortō

'Modern art!' beamed Caecilius, as three workers man-handled the TARDIS into a corner. He was a tall, cheerful man with a big heart, full of joy for life. Right now, his joy was squarely aimed at the strange blue box he had just bought for a very reasonable price. He smiled at it, marvelling at how well suited it was for the room.

The villa was a big, open-plan design, with a large atrium and living area leading off to smaller alcoves. Four large hypocaust grilles in the floor constantly pumped out thick gusts of hot steam. There were vases, plants, busts, statues and gaudy chunks of decorative marble everywhere. Caecilius was a man who liked art, the fancier the better. But there was something about this blue box that intrigued him more than anything. He'd always admired modern art, especially the way it was occasionally hard to tell what was actually art and what was just a weird lump of material. It was a matter of will, sometimes. If you said something was art, and said it loudly enough, people would believe it, even if it looked like a child had made it; especially so in some cases. Plenty of modern art was undeniably beautiful, of course, but it was all subjective in the end. As long as you liked something, and it gave you pleasure, then it was art, and nobody could tell you otherwise.

This, though. This strange blue box. This was special. Somehow it simultaneously looked both out of place and also like it was made specifically for the villa. As if its inevitable destination had always been that exact corner at that exact moment in time. Caecilius had a feeling that it would fit in perfectly anywhere, no matter the setting. It belonged, yet clearly didn't belong, so your eyes just passed right over it, until you took a closer look. He'd never seen anything quite like it.

'That's it, just there,' he said, as the workmen settled the box neatly into the corner. He turned to the Major Domo, the head of the household. 'Rhombus, I'm a bit peckish, can you get me some ants in honey, there's a good lad. Oh, and maybe a dormouse?'

He noticed his wife, Metella, hovering, throwing a suspicious look at the box, and his 17-year-old daughter, Evelina, watching from the back of the room. He pointed at his new purchase, proudly. 'Well? What do you think?'

Metella was unimpressed. She didn't see the point in most of the decorative flourishes in the villa, although she was rather partial to a cornice. 'You call it modern art, I call it a blooming great waste of space.'

'But we're going up in the world,' enthused Caecilius. 'Lucius Dextrus himself is coming here, this very afternoon! What with that, and our Evelina, about to be elevated—'

'Oh, don't go on about it, Dad,' said Evelina, embarrassed at the attention. She stared at the box, slightly mesmerised, as if by a memory she'd forgotten. She blinked, tearing her gaze away from it, clearing her head.

'If we'd moved to Rome like I said, she could have been a Vestal Virgin,' said Metella.

Caecilius, all too familiar with this refrain, mouthed the words along with her – but very carefully, so that she didn't catch him doing it.

Quintus, their 18-year-old son, walked in, yawning. 'Somebody mention Vestal Virgins?'

'Quintus!' said Metella. 'Don't be so rude! You apologise to the Household Gods, this instant!'

Quintus rolled his eyes. 'Oh get off. I had too much wine last night, my head is a bit delicate for all this.'

'You apologise, right now! The gods are always watching!'

As if on cue, an earthquake started shaking the house. Metella threw her arms out, vindicated, raising her eyebrows at Quintus.

'You see?' she said. 'Look what you've done!'

'Positions!' yelled Caecilius. They all ran to prear-ranged places, ready to catch anything in a precarious position. Everything shook. Metella caught a vase as it tumbled off a plinth, Evelina caught another vase, Caecilius threw his arms around some amphorae, and Quintus just held his head, as if it were in more danger of shattering than any of the ornaments.

The tremors faded away, and the family carefully put everything back in their places. Metella pointed at Quintus, who had been absolutely no help at all. 'There now, you've made the heavens angry! Say sorry! I tell you, Caecilius, that boy will do no good.'

Quintus sighed, and stomped over to an alcove. On one wall, there was a small bas-relief sculpture of a god and a goddess in a temple, household guardians called Lares. Sitting on a small shelf in front, there was a decorative goblet of wine. Quintus dipped his fingers into the wine, and sprinkled some drops onto the sculpture. He muttered, embarrassed at having to do it, 'Sorry, Household Gods . . .' He didn't really believe that anyone was watching over them, and if they were, he certainly didn't think they'd care whether or not he splashed a bit of wine on a tiny sculpture. But his parents believed it, and so did Evelina, so he went along with it for a quiet life. Quintus was all about the easy, simple path, quite happy to coast through life for the moment. And, right now, his thumping headache demanded a particularly quiet life and didn't need any arguments. His work done for the day, Quintus slumped onto a nearby couch, holding his forehead.

Caecilius marched over to him, disappointed at his behaviour. 'And where were you last night?' he asked. 'Down the thermopolium, I bet. Cavorting with Etruscans and Christians and all sorts.'

'Yes, and I've got quite a spectacular headache, obviously, so if you could please stop shouting—'

'Oh, I know a song about headaches! Would you like to hear it?'

Quintus tried to wave him away, he knew what was coming. 'No, please no . . .'

Caecilius started 'singing', which just consisted of him clapping loudly while shouting 'LA LA LA LA LA LA' at Quintus. Quintus groaned in pain, his head throbbing at the noise.

'All right, Dad! Give us a break!'

Metella was disappointed. 'You want to smarten yourself up, Quintus. Before Lucius Dextrus gets here, but in general, too. You want to be more like your sister, look. She's giving us status!'

'Oh, because it's all about Evelina,' mumbled Quintus.

'You should be proud of your sister, for once. She has the gift!' Metella held up Evelina's hand to show Quintus. There was a detailed eye painted on the back of it, and a matching one on the back of her other hand.

Metella looked at Evelina, concerned. 'Have you been consuming?'

Evelina shook her head. 'Not this morning.'

'Come on, sweetheart, practise.'

She led Evelina over to one of the grilles, which was steaming more forcefully than the others.

'It's hot today,' said Metella. 'The hypocaust is on full blast. The mountain god must be happy. Breathe deeply. Remember what the Sisterhood said.'

Evelina leaned into the hot vapour and started breathing it in. She closed her eyes, struggling to keep her face in the steam. 'It hurts.'

'Oh, my love, is it too hot?'

Evelina looked troubled. 'It's not that. It hurts inside. In my mind. Sometimes, in the smoke, I see the most terrible things.'

'Like what?'

'A face. A face of stone.'

Metella worried for Evelina. She had to trust the Sisterhood, they'd never been wrong before. But this didn't seem right. Evelina looked pale and drawn, haunted by the things she could see. Discovering that she had the gift of sight had been exciting at first, until the weight of some of the visions began to drag her down. She was still so young, she shouldn't have to face the future yet – but she saw it every day, whether she wanted to or not. Then there was her arm, which was getting worse every day. Whatever this process was,

Metella hoped it would be over soon. She wanted her happy, funny daughter back. It had been a long time since she'd heard her laugh, or even seen her smile.

In most respects, they were a normal, happy family. Bumbling along through life, doing the best they could, trying to do the right thing, enjoying their hobbies, coping with work, and loving each other. But Evelina's special abilities had changed the course of their lives, and made things more complicated.

'It'll make sense one day,' said Metella. 'Sister Spurrina promised. The veil will be parted. You'll be a Seer.'

Evelina breathed the fumes in deeply. As the steam surrounded her, she saw the face again. A dark face of stone, with eyes of blazing fire.

Evelina opened her eyes. 'Who are you?' she whispered.

Nobody answered her. The face was gone.

Chapter IV

Sub rosa

The Temple of Sibyl shook as the ground rumbled. It was a huge, ornate building, with elaborate decorations, columns and hanging tapestries. It was the home of a group of Soothsayers with psychic powers, who followed the prophecies of the oracle Sibyl. Although these days, they came up with their own prophecies.

And every single one was completely accurate.

Mira the Soothsayer ran into the temple, unconcerned by the earthquake. Her gift of sight meant she knew she was safe, the ground would stop shaking in a few minutes. She'd known it was about to start, and which market stalls she'd need to dodge when they collapsed. She had bigger things to worry about. The tall man and the loud woman were here in Pompeii, with their blue box, right out of the prophecy. Although this wasn't one of the recent predictions, it was from their sacred texts. Those tended to be more . . . open to interpretation. They were written before the gift of sight had touched them all. Now there was never any doubt. You couldn't fake a vision or a prediction here, everyone would know, or find out soon enough. Gifts from the gods. Although sometimes it felt less like a gift and more like a curse. Some people didn't want to know everything that was going to happen. What was the point of free will, if everything was predestined, if you were simply following some course of action that someone else had seen? She wasn't even sure herself. But these were blasphemous thoughts, rarely spoken aloud. The kind of thoughts that could get you killed.

The blue box prediction appeared to have come true, though, and that meant that they were in danger. Everyone was.

Mira ran through the building, out of breath, past the columns and red curtains. Several female guards stood on duty, carrying fearsome spears. None of them challenged her. She was the youngest of them all, here, but she was one of the family. She went where she pleased.

She ran into the main chamber and prostrated herself before the Sisters. The Sibylline Sisterhood. Several women sitting together, surrounded by religious displays and animal skulls, with a fire pit in front of them. Their leader – Mira's imperious confidante on her journey through the market – stepped forward. Spurrina had devoted her life to the Sisterhood and had the pure confidence that can only come from always being right. She had never been unsure about anything in her life.

She cast a disdainful glance at Mira, who was breathing heavily, and had clearly run all the way here. This was undignified, particularly in the presence of the gods.

'I beg audience with the High Priestess of the Sibylline,' said the Soothsayer, trying to settle herself.

'The High Priestess cannot be seen,' said Spurrina. 'What would you tell her, Sister?'

'About the box!'

Another Soothsayer, Thalina, stepped forward. 'You have already been told,' she hissed. 'That prophecy is no longer part of our belief. It is an outdated text, from before our eyes were opened. We have new prophecies now. We are guided by the gods themselves.'

'But I have seen it,' said Mira. 'I have seen the box. And the travellers with it. They speak strange words. Their thoughts twist like snakes. They are not of Pompeii. They are not of us.'

'Then what does it matter?' said Spurrina. 'Travellers know nothing of our world. Pay them no heed, and keep your mind clear. We have bigger concerns than tourists and wanderers.'

'But Sisters, I—'

'Do not question your Sisters!' interrupted Thalina. 'You would do well to listen and learn.'

Spurrina raised a hand to stop Thalina. 'The others are already looking for the original prophecy,' she said. 'When we find it, you will see how out of date it is.'

Thalina scoffed. 'You humour her too much, I fear. She has too many ideas. Thinks entirely too much.'

'It does no harm to make sure,' said Spurrina. 'That way, we can set all our minds to rest, before the others start talking and worrying.'

Mira felt it would take a lot to set *her* mind at rest. Her Sisters hadn't heard the strangers' conversation, seen their animated faces, as they spoke of frightening things that made no sense. Some sort of disaster. A lot of dead people. Were they visions? Or were they plotting to cause the deaths? No, the loud one seemed insistent on preventing death, that looked to be the cause of the argument. They talked so much, using far more words than necessary, it had been difficult to keep track of what they said. They didn't make a lot of sense.

Until the tall one had called the loud one 'a silly old soothsayer'. Mira understood those words perfectly well.

People had once used the same sort of language to mock the Sisters, and all the other augurs of the city – until they started making accurate predictions. Then suddenly people couldn't get enough of them. They gained huge respect almost overnight, were fast-tracked into positions of power and influence, and were now revered. But Mira never forgot how things used to be. Even though she had only been five years old when things changed, she had very clear memories of it.

Children see more than most adults realise, they pick up on moods and expressions, because they're still learning and developing emotions, taking their behavioural cues from others. Mira was always very perceptive, especially as a child, and saw it all. The looks her family would get, the jokes, the sympathetic glances, the hostility. She recognised an unbeliever when she saw one. The look on the tall man's face spoke volumes.

'The tall one,' Mira said softly. 'He thinks of us as figures of ridicule.'

'Then he is a stranger to Pompeii,' replied Spurrina. 'Soon he will learn.'

Just then, there was a commotion from the chambers at the back. Several of the other Sisters were talking animatedly, some happy, some upset. Thalina hurried over to see what was going on.

'What's all this fuss?' said Spurrina. 'They'll wake the High Priestess if they're not careful. Sisters!'

The others tried to lower their voices, but were too excited. Thalina came back out, and beckoned to Spurrina urgently. 'They have found it, Sister Spurrina! In the Thirteenth Book of the Sibylline Oracles. The blue box. A temple made of wood.'

Spurrina and Mira walked with Thalina over to a table, where another of the Sisterhood had unrolled an ancient scroll. One of the original prophecies of Sibyl. They stared at it, reverently. Among the words and pictures, there was a crude but distinct drawing of a blue box.

Mira pointed excitedly. 'That's it!' she said. 'It is exactly as I saw!' She felt vindicated at last. Spending the morning running around chasing the strangers had been worth it after all.

'Mira is right,' said Thalina. 'And yet the Sibyl foretold that the box would appear at the time of storms, fire and betrayal. We have seen nothing of this. How can this be so accurate, but all the other parts so different?'

'Sisters,' wheezed a hoarse, guttural voice, startling them all. They turned to look.

Behind the altar, on a pile of cushions and blankets, the High Priestess sat behind a curtain, shielded from view, backlit by candles, just a silhouette. She struggled to sit up, slowly, in considerable pain. She slept most of the day lately, so this activity was unusual for her. In fact, her condition meant she rarely intervened in their daily routine at all, she was too weak. The blessings of the gods had taken a heavy toll, just as they would eventually do to the rest of them. The price was high, but well worth paying. This was their destiny.

The High Priestess called out to the others again, her voice cracking with the effort. 'Sisters!'

Spurrina hurried over to her, worried. 'Reverend Mother, you should sleep.'

'The Sibylline Oracles are wrong,' said the High Priestess.

Spurrina looked flummoxed. 'But we have venerated the Sibyl's words for generations. We adapted, of course, we retired some of the predictions, but her words have always been the foundation of our beliefs. And now we know she has predicted the arrival of this strange blue box, along with the travellers. The Oracles cannot all be wrong, surely?'

'This is a new age,' said the High Priestess, seeming to gain strength from her words. 'Heed my words. I predict a future of prosperity and might. An endless empire of Pompeii, reaching out from this city to topple Rome itself and encompass the whole, wide world. If the disciples of the blue box defy this prophecy, their blood will run across the temple floor!'

Mira jumped as the ground began to shake just as the High Priestess finished speaking, another tremor rattling the temple.

Spurrina looked around, pleased by this auspicious sign. 'The gods approve,' she said.

Everyone else looked happy, too. Except for Mira. That nagging, gut feeling was back. For the first time in her life, she was asking herself a question that scared her: what if her Sisters were wrong?

Chapter V

Prima facie

The Doctor and Donna walked towards what looked like Caecilius's villa, hoping that they were in the right place. They'd been told he worked in the marble trade, and that it would be obvious which one was his home. This villa was completely covered in marble, so there was no question about that. Whoever lived here was clearly a big marble fan. There were marble statues, marble paving stones, marble cats and marble dogs. There were even some marble trees, carefully carved and sculpted, dotted about between the real trees. It was right on the border between tasteful and 1970s Las Vegas, although even Liberace might have said this was a little bit over the top.

'Let me do the talking,' said the Doctor, as they got closer to the entrance. 'If that's at all possible.'

'I'll do some punching in a minute,' said Donna, glaring at him.

'Just . . . try not to be weird with them.'

'Me?! You forget people are real sometimes! You're the weird one, you . . . weird spaceman weirdo.'

'Oh, great comeback, maybe you should do the talking after all.'

'You can put a sock in it, sunshine, I'm not in the mood. I'm ready to explode, a bit like that gigantic volcano that's about to pop.'

'I told you, don't mention that!'

'Why not?'

'Because that word hasn't been invented yet!'

'I know,' said Donna. 'But surely—'

'No. It'll start too many questions. The quicker we go, the quicker we'll get out of here. Less talky, more walky.'

'You are absolutely—'

She was interrupted by a loud crack, and a low rumbling. Another earthquake was starting.

'Positions!' they heard someone yell from the villa.

Inside, the family sprang into action for the second time that day.

'Quick!' shouted Caecilius.

'Oh no, not again . . .' muttered Quintus, protecting his goblet of wine.

Everyone ran around to catch the vases, amphorae, and potted plants, just like before. Unlike before, they'd been caught unawares, in different parts of the villa. Quintus was no use. Near the front entrance, a marble bust tipped over, just before Caecilius could get to it. He watched, distraught, as it toppled off the plinth, tumbling towards the floor—

Only to be caught by a tall man in strange, close-fitting clothes, who was suddenly standing next to it.

'Whoa! There you go!' said the newcomer, placing the bust carefully back on its plinth.

Then the earthquake rumbled to a halt, and the shaking stopped.

'Thank you, kind sir,' Caecilius began, 'but I'm afraid business is closed for the day. I'm expecting a visitor.'

'That's me! I'm a visitor! Hello!' The man gestured to a startled woman with red hair and Celtic looks who'd come up behind him. 'And so is she. Apologies for her in advance.'

'You'll be sorry for something,' the Celt assured him.

The tall man tried to speak again, but Caecilius cut him off as two workers hurried inside with a long, thin slab of marble. 'Just over there, please,' he said, watching anxiously as they hefted it around. 'Thank goodness you didn't drop it. Be careful!'

'What's that?' Metella exclaimed.

'You can see what it is,' Caecilius told Metella. 'It's going to be a table for Tiberius.'

'I hope he's paying you, this time,' said Metella. 'And not in fruit baskets again. It's going to be there all day, is it?'

'Very probably. Quintus, can you wake up? I need to move that chair.'

'Please stop shouting, Dad.'

'OI!EVERYBODYSHUUUUUTUUUUUUUP!'

Quintus clutched at his ears at the Celtic woman's fiery cry. Finally, there was silence, as the echoes of her voice faded.

'Blimey,' said the man in the close-fitting clothes, grinning. 'That's better. I don't know how you lot ever got any roads built.'

The family looked blankly at the new arrivals.

'Sorry, who are you again?' asked Caecilius.

'I am . . . Spartacus,' said Spartacus, seeming to find this incredibly amusing.

'And so am I!' announced the Celt, grinning widely.

For a moment, there was complete silence.

'Mr and Mrs Spartacus?' said Caecilius.

'Oh, no no no – we're not . . . we're not married,' said Spartacus hastily.

'We're not even together,' said the woman quickly. 'Not at all. That is a big old nope, thank you very much.'

'Oh,' said Caecilius. 'So you're brother and sister? Yes, of course! You do look very much alike.'

The newcomers looked at each other, baffled.

'Really?' said Spartacus.

'Yeah, really? I mean, *really*?' said his sister.

'All right,' said Spartacus. 'You don't have to sound

quite so horrified. This is a good face, one of my best. Then again, I would say that.'

'Well it's very nice to meet you, but as I said, I'm not open for trade today,' said Caecilius.

'And that trade would be . . . ?'

'Marble! The mining, polishing and design thereof. My name is Lobus Caecilius. If you want marble, I'm your man!'

Spartacus nodded, and then whipped out a small piece of fine parchment. 'That's good,' he said, waving the document around airily. 'Because I'm . . . the marble inspector.'

For a moment, just a split second, Caecilius could have sworn that the parchment was blank. He blinked, and realised that he must have been mistaken. It was official confirmation that not only was this man the marble inspector, he was the Chief Marble Inspector for this entire region, with a particular interest in detecting any fraudulent objects containing fake marble. This was serious. Caecilius's mouth opened and closed several times, like a goldfish, but no sound came out.

Metella sprang into action. 'By the gods of commerce, an inspection! I'm so sorry sir, I do apologise for my son.' She grabbed Quintus's goblet and poured away the wine.

'Oi!' said Quintus, looking heartbroken.

'This is my good wife, Metella,' said Caecilius, finally snapping out of his shock. 'I must confess, we're not prepared for an inspection, we're closed today, to complete a special order—'

'Nothing to worry about,' said the Inspector. 'All friends here. Why don't you just call me Doctor? Bit less confusing for everyone. And she's Donna.'

'Donna Spartacus,' said Donna with a pout.

'We're sure you've got nothing to hide,' the Doctor went on, striding towards the blue box Caecilius had just bought. 'Although frankly, that object looks rather like wood to me . . .'

'I told you to get rid of it!' hissed Metella.

'I only bought it today!'

'Ah well, *caveat emptor*,' said the Doctor.

Caecilius looked at him. 'Oh, you're Celtic, too,' he said. 'There's lovely.'

'I'm sure it's fine,' said the Doctor. 'But I might have to take it off your hands for a proper inspection. We'll bring it back if it all looks shipshape.'

'Won't you stay for a spot of early lunch? As our honoured guests?' Caecilius hoped they'd say no, this was already a little awkward, but if it helped the inspection to go a bit more smoothly, he was willing to give it a try.

'We really must be going as soon as we're finished,' said the Doctor.

'Such a shame!' said Caecilius, relieved.

'Couldn't hurt though, could it?' said Donna, hanging back. 'Meet the people, get to know the faces behind the names? See how they *live*?'

'No,' said the Doctor, widening his eyes at her. 'As I said, we've really got to be going, haven't we, Ulterious Motivus?'

'I suppose so, Pompous Gittius.'

'Biggius Mouthius.'

'Gluteus Maximus.'

They stopped when they noticed the others staring at them, baffled. The Doctor flashed a big smile that didn't seem completely genuine. 'Tell you what, you go and have your lunch, we'll finish up here and let ourselves out. We don't want to be any trouble.'

This was good news to Caecilius, although the other inspector was being difficult for some reason.

Donna spoke quite pointedly. 'Although while we're here, wouldn't you recommend a nice holiday, Spartacus?'

'Don't know what you mean, Spartacus.'

'This lovely family. Don't you think they should get out of town for a few days? Like, right now?'

This was all getting too weird for Caecilius. 'Why should we do that?'

Donna did a double take. 'Well, the volcano, for starters.'

Caecilius, Metella and Quintus looked completely blank.

'The what?' said Caecilius.

'The volcano!'

'The what-ano?'

55

'The great big volcano right on your doorstep!'

The Doctor grabbed Donna, as if he was trying to keep her quiet. 'For shame, Spartacus! We haven't greeted the Household Gods yet! 'Scuse us, just be a moment!'

As the family continued talking and clearing up the room, the Doctor frogmarched Donna over to the alcove, and sprinkled wine over the display of the Household Gods, muttering quietly.

'I told you,' he said, 'stop using the v-word! They don't have any idea what that is. Vesuvius is just a mountain to them. The top hasn't blown off yet.'

'Listen, I don't know what sort of kids you've been flying around with in outer space, but you're not telling me to shut up.' Donna pointed at Quintus. 'That boy, how old is he? Sixteen? And tomorrow, he burns to death.'

'And that's my fault?'

'Right now, yes! So we can't warn everyone, but we can still save them. Get them out with the TARDIS, they don't even need to know why. We could evacuate the whole city. By force, if we have to, you can probably scoop them up without them even realising.'

The Doctor frowned. 'No, we can't, of course we can't. It's forbidden by the Laws of Time. This is a historical event, it happened, it cannot un-happen. If I pull out this one thread, the entire tapestry of history unravels.'

56

'So? They can make a new one. Send me the bill. Good luck chasing the payments, I'm blacklisted from three credit card companies.'

'Donna, there are forces at work greater than you could possibly imagine.'

'Behold,' said Donna, gesturing at a small pot plant and orating dramatically, as if giving a speech. 'The tiny field in which I grow my cares. Lay thine eyes upon it, and thou shalt see that it is barren.'

'. . . What?'

'I don't give a monkey's.'

'You don't understand,' said the Doctor. 'If everything comes unravelled, then the very fabric of space and time will be ripped apart.'

'What's with all the fabric and tapestry metaphors?' asked Donna.

The Doctor blinked, taken aback. 'I dunno, that's how it was explained to me. It *is* a bit odd, now you mention it. More visual, I suppose. They got a blanket out, put fruits on it, and – anyway, the point is, I can't interfere.'

Donna snorted a laugh. 'You interfere all the time! You love it! "Interfering" would be your middle name, if you had a proper name like a real person. "The Interfering Doctor". Look at these people. They're not history. You said it yourself, relative to my present day or not, right now they're alive. Look at them! Go on, I said look!'

The Doctor reluctantly glanced over. The family were laughing at something, some private joke. Affectionate. Loving. Alive. Doomed. He looked away, haunted.

'I can't.'

Donna shook her head, bemused. 'Laws of Time, honestly . . . Are they written down? In a special book?'

The Doctor hesitated. Probably. 'Somewhere, yes.'

Donna suddenly clicked her fingers triumphantly. She had thought of a loophole. 'Aha! Wait! What about that marble thing? You caught it when we walked in. That would have fallen on the ground and smashed otherwise. You've already interfered! Checkmate, mate!'

The Doctor thought about it. 'That . . . might not have broken, it could have been fine without me.'

'Oh, OK then, how about we go knock it over again, see what happens? If it bounces, fine, if it breaks, then we're OK to save everyone?'

'No! Look, we're not here to change history. We're here to preserve it.'

'Yeah, and it will be preserved. Forever. In ash. From the eruption that kills everyone tomorrow.'

The Doctor was very quiet. 'There's nothing we can do,' he said.

Caecilius was just about giving up hope that the strange visitors would ever leave, when the Major Domo walked in, and bellowed: 'Announcing Lucius Petrus Dextrus, Chief Augur of the City Government.'

Lucius strode in, head held high, as if he owned the place. He was an imposing man in his fifties, with a constant sneer on his face, and a cruel remark never far from his lips. His right arm was covered in robes, held tightly against his body, looking as if he had hurt himself. He was flanked by two Roman soldiers, the bodyguards adding to his apparent sense of importance. It was quite an entrance, all pomp and circumstance. Caecilius wouldn't have been surprised if there had been a few trumpeters walking respectfully behind him, playing a little fanfare. He was sure if he suggested it, next time Lucius appeared there would be a full brass section following him around.

He did have considerable power and influence, though, and Caecilius immediately deferred to him. 'Lucius! My pleasure, as always.'

'Quintus, stand up,' said Metella. Even she looked nervous at being near Lucius. Caecilius wasn't surprised. There was something about Lucius that bothered him, something cold and hard in his eyes. He held considerable sway in the city, so it made sense to keep on his good side. Mostly because nobody wanted to find out what happened if you got on his bad side.

Caecilius continued bowing and scraping magnificently. 'A rare and great honour, sir, for you to come to my house.'

He tried to shake hands, but Lucius kept his arm firmly where it was. Caecilius slowly withdrew his hand, embarrassed.

'The birds are flying north, and the wind is in the west,' pronounced Lucius, as if that explained everything.

'Quite,' said Caecilius, trying to follow along with it. 'Absolutely. That's good, is it?'

'Only the grain of wheat knows where it will grow,' continued Lucius, in the manner of someone who had grown accustomed to never being questioned or corrected.

'There now, Metella, have you ever heard such wisdom?' said Caecilius.

'Never!' she replied. Caecilius was pretty sure she had no idea what Lucius was talking about either, but neither of them was going to admit it while he was standing right there. 'It's an honour.'

Caecilius suddenly remembered the strange visitors, and gestured to them. 'Pardon me, sir, I have guests – or rather, inspectors. This is Spartacus, and, er, Spartacus.'

In the alcove, the Doctor and Donna realised everyone was now looking at them. They stepped out, greeting the new arrival, waving. Lucius looked them up and down disdainfully. 'You're both called Spartacus?'

'Apparently,' said the Doctor, making a face at Donna.

'Although I'm definitely going to stick to "John Smith" in future.' He looked at Lucius, taking the measure of him. The Doctor could always spot a bully, usually with one quick glance. Something in the haughty expression, the arrogant stance, the expectation that everyone else would just do as they said. The Doctor didn't like bullies. At all. He did, however, very much enjoy taking them down a peg or three. Even better if he could make a fool of them at the same time. Bullies hated being laughed at, possibly more than they hated those they preyed upon. They were essentially cowards, and the trouble with being a bully was that, sooner or later, a bigger, stronger kid would come along and whack you on the nose.

'A name is but a cloud upon the summer wind,' said Lucius, quickly trying to establish dominance over the unexpected guests.

The Doctor smiled, immediately firing a shot back. 'But the wind is felt most keenly in the dark.'

'Ah!' exclaimed Lucius. 'But what is the dark, other than an omen of the sun?'

'I concede that every sun must set,' said the Doctor, making Lucius bark out a victorious laugh. But the Doctor had a trump card to play: 'And yet the son of the father must also rise.'

'Damn,' said Lucius, annoyed but impressed. 'Very clever, sir. Evidently, a man of learning.'

'Oh, yes,' said the Doctor. 'But don't mind me. Don't want to disturb the status quo.'

Lucius looked at him sharply.

'He's Celtic,' Caecilius explained.

Lucius shrugged, looking bored of the small talk. He turned to Caecilius. 'Is it ready?'

'All complete, sir! Just over here.' Caecilius led Lucius over to a plinth, with a cloth draped over it, hiding something underneath.

'We'll be off in a minute, anyway,' said the Doctor. It was time to make a quiet exit, they'd been here more than long enough. He tried to lead Donna over to the TARDIS, getting his key out, but she was trying to lead him right back, causing a very polite, quiet shoving match.

'I'm not going!' muttered Donna.

'Yes, we are,' said the Doctor. 'That vol- that mountain is ready to blow, I can't stop it, and there is absolutely nothing that will change my mind . . .' He trailed off as Caecilius pulled the cloth away, proudly revealing his work.

On top of the plinth was something that looked very out of place in ancient Pompeii. At first glance, it was simply a thin, square piece of marble, with several patterns carved into it.

But to the visitors from the future, it looked exactly like an electronic circuit board.

Chapter VI

Quid pro quo

Donna stared at the stone circuit board, confused at the bizarre intrusion of modern electronics into this ancient setting. She didn't protest as the Doctor pulled her forward for a closer look. As they walked, Donna bumped into the marble bust that the Doctor had saved earlier. It fell to the floor, and smashed into several pieces. Everyone looked at them, startled.

'Sorry!' said Donna. 'My fault. I'll get you another one.'

'Don't worry, I've got a job lot of them out the back,' said Caecilius quickly. 'They've all got imperfections, so I picked them up for a bargain. That one had a wonky ear, looked like a fish. The ear looked like a fish, I mean, not the whole thing.'

Lucius's face clouded over at the interruption. 'If we could return to the matter at hand,' he said. Caecilius nodded, and they carried on talking.

Donna raised her eyebrows at the Doctor. 'Well hey, what a surprise, looks like it would have broken after all,' she whispered, pointing at the broken pieces of the marble bust. 'So you already *did* interfere.'

The Doctor stared at her suspiciously. 'Did you knock it over on purpose?'

Donna tried to look extremely shocked at the mere suggestion, placing a hand over her heart innocently. 'What an outrageous and untrue allegation, I'm stunned that you would even accuse me of such a thing! I would never, *ever* do anything like that . . . Unless I knew I was right all along, which I totally was.'

'Doesn't mean anything. Doesn't mean we can get involved.'

'No,' said Donna, grinning. She pointed at the marble circuit board. 'But I think that does.'

The Doctor rolled his eyes. 'You're very annoying when you're wrong about something, but so much worse when you're right. I can't believe you just vandalised the place to prove a point.'

Donna shrugged, unrepentant. 'You should see me on a quiz night.'

They casually strolled over to where Caecilius was showing off to Lucius.

'Exactly as you specified,' said Caecilius, waving his arms around the circuit board as if he was presenting the star prize on a TV game show. 'If it pleases you?'

Lucius inspected it, then nodded in satisfaction, comparing it to a parchment design sketch. 'As the rain pleases the soil.'

'Now that's different,' said the Doctor, walking around it in a circle, examining it. 'Who designed that, then?'

'My Lord Lucius was very specific,' said Caecilius.

'Yeah, didn't seem like your usual sort of thing,' said the Doctor.

Donna raised an eyebrow. 'Looks like a circuit to me.'

'Made of stone,' said the Doctor. 'But we're a couple of thousand years too early for that, there's no way you invented it out of the blue and everyone just forgot about it. Where'd you get the pattern from?'

'On the rain and mist and wind,' intoned Lucius.

Donna wasn't sure what was going on here, but it couldn't be a coincidence. She looked at Lucius, and back at the circuit board again. 'Come off it. You mean you just dreamt that up, all by yourself?'

'That is my job, as City Augur,' said Lucius.

'What's that, then, like the mayor?'

'You must excuse my friend, she's from Barcelona,' said the Doctor. He spoke more quietly to Donna. 'This is an age of superstition. The Augur tells the future, it's his job. When he says something like "the wind will blow from the west", that's the equivalent of the ten o'clock news. But this is way beyond simple predictions, the very idea of an electronic circuit would have seemed like pure magic to them. If you showed them a digital watch, they'd probably worship it as a deity.'

Evelina walked in, looking at the Doctor and Donna. She seemed as if she'd been drugged, pale and swaying, unsteady on her feet, eyes in shadow. She looked ill.

'They're laughing at us,' she said, pointing at them. 'Those two. They use words like tricksters. They're mocking us.'

Donna glanced at the Doctor. Something wasn't right here. At all. She was suddenly very aware of how dangerous life was in this era, how quickly they could get themselves into trouble. They were very much outnumbered, even if you didn't count the two Roman soldiers and their extremely sharp swords.

'We meant no offence,' said the Doctor. 'We're new to this area, still learning all the customs.'

'I'm sorry,' said Metella. 'My daughter's been consuming the vapours.'

Quintus stepped forward, shocked at his sister's pallid appearance. 'Gods, Mother, what have you been doing to her? She's sick! Just look at her.'

Lucius looked at Evelina as if she was an insect. 'I gather I have a rival in this household. Another with the gift.'

Metella beamed, proud of her daughter. 'She's been promised to the Sibylline Sisterhood. They say she has remarkable visions.'

Lucius looked almost disgusted. 'The prophecies of

women are limited and dull,' he scoffed. 'Only the menfolk have the capacity for true perception.'

Donna raised an eyebrow at Lucius, highly unimpressed with his attitude. 'I'll tell you where the wind's blowing right now, mate.'

Just as she said it, there was another light rumble from Vesuvius. It rattled the vases, and sounded almost threatening.

Lucius smiled at Donna smugly. 'The mountain god marks your words. You would be advised to mark them also.'

The Doctor looked more closely at Evelina's drawn, pale face. 'What do you mean, consuming the vapours? From the hypocaust?' he asked.

Evelina turned her gaunt gaze upon him. 'They give me strength.'

'Doesn't look like it to me,' said the Doctor.

'Is that your opinion . . . as a *doctor*?' said Evelina pointedly.

The words hit the Doctor like a lightning bolt. He stared at Evelina, who stared right back. Donna was surprised too. Evelina had only just walked in, and couldn't know their real names.

'I beg your pardon?' said the Doctor, feeling a slight chill despite the heat from the vents.

'Doctor,' said Evelina. 'That's your name.'

'How did you know that?'

But Evelina had turned towards Donna now. 'And you. You call yourself Noble.'

Donna was startled, but Evelina wasn't trying to impress them, or hurt them. It looked like the words were pouring out of her like the sweat on her forehead. She seemed powerless to stop herself speaking, in fact it was as if it would hurt if she tried to. She just had to stand there and let the words spill out. The more she spoke, the more ill she looked.

'Now then, Evelina, don't be rude,' said Metella, scared.

'No, no, let her talk,' said the Doctor, fascinated.

Evelina faced the Doctor and Donna, looking right through them as if they weren't even there, as if she was staring at something beyond them. She was having a vision. It consumed her. 'You both come from so far away,' she said.

Lucius snorted, annoyed. 'The female soothsayer is inclined to invent all sorts of vagaries, embellishing the truth with flowery tales.'

'Oh, not this time, Lucius,' said the Doctor. 'I reckon this time, you've been out-soothsayed.'

Lucius glared at the Doctor. His facial expression indicated that he had a few tricks of his own up his sleeve. 'Is that so . . . man from Gallifrey?'

The Doctor jolted, as if he'd been given an electric shock. 'What?'

Now Donna and the Doctor really were at a

disadvantage. At first, it had seemed as if Evelina was the only one with inside knowledge, but Lucius was clearly on the same, secret inside track. It felt like a pincer movement, one on each side, trapping them with their words.

'The strangest of images,' continued Lucius, enjoying himself, but particularly enjoying their discomfiture. 'Your home is lost in fire, is it not?'

'Doctor, what are they doing?' asked Donna, but the Doctor was temporarily lost for words. The room felt much smaller suddenly, hotter, more intense, like they had been inside a newly formed volcano all along without realising that the heat and intensity had slowly been rising. They were suddenly very out of their depth, and the Doctor looked completely shaken. Donna had never seen him like this; normally he was full of confidence, happy to bluff and bluster, but this wasn't like him at all.

'And you,' said Lucius, looking at Donna, making her jump. 'Daughter of . . . London.'

Donna was very, very frightened now. They were supposed to be the ones with all the information, this wasn't possible. 'How does he know that?'

'The gift of Pompeii,' said Lucius. 'Every oracle tells the truth.'

'That's impossible,' said Donna.

'You merely came along for the journey,' said Lucius. 'Following this man like a lost pet. Or a father figure? You have lost yours recently. Your world is basic, lonely and functional. You work in small buildings for small people, living your small life. You were more useful as food for the spiders, you should have let them take you. Perhaps they will try again one day.'

'Doctor . . . ?' said Donna, but he looked as lost as she did.

Evelina had one more bombshell to drop. She walked over to the Doctor, the vision coursing through her, eyes dancing with the fire from the candles.

'Even the word "Doctor" is false,' she said. 'Your real name is hidden. It burns in the stars. In the Cascade of Medusa herself. You are a Lord, sir. A Lord of Time.'

Her eyelids fluttered, she stumbled, and fainted.

In her bedroom, Evelina slept, pale and restless. Metella watched over her, worried, adjusting a large bandage on Evelina's arm.

Donna walked in. 'Is she all right? That was pretty intense.'

'She's resting now,' said Metella. 'She didn't mean to be rude, she's ever such a good girl. But when the gods speak through her, she has no control over what she sees. It's the gift. It doesn't always make sense, not in any way we can work out. I'm sorry, I hope she didn't upset you both.'

Donna waved away her apology. 'Don't worry about that. What's wrong with her arm?'

'An irritation of the skin. She never complains, bless her. We bathe it in olive oil every night, but it doesn't help much.'

'The skin? What is it, a burn or something?' asked Donna.

Metella hesitated. 'Please,' she said. 'Evelina said you'd come from far away, and you travel with a doctor. Could you take a look? If I wasn't so worried, I'd never have mentioned it, but something tells me I can trust you both. You dress so differently, your words are so strange. You seem to know things that are beyond our understanding.'

'Of course, let me see,' said Donna.

Metella unwrapped the bandage from Evelina's arm. There was a large rash, a patch of dusty, dry skin, almost grey. 'Have you ever seen anything like it?'

Donna touched it, and flakes came away in her fingers. She looked closely. It was stone.

Evelina's arm was turning to stone.

Donna was shocked into silence. At school, she'd learned all about what happened in Pompeii, how the eruption had buried and preserved all the people who lived there, as the ash hardened. Eventually, the bodies decayed, leaving holes inside the solid ash. Almost 2,000 years later, Italian archaeologist Giuseppe Fiorelli discovered the body-shaped holes, poured liquid plaster inside, waited for it to harden, then chipped away the surrounding ash to reveal perfect plaster casts

71

of the victims. It was a stunning, unprecedented look into the lives and deaths of the residents of Pompeii.

Right now, though, Donna was surrounded by the real people who lived here. They weren't plaster casts; they were living, breathing human beings, with hopes, dreams, plans and voices. She expected to find it difficult to face them, but she didn't expect to see one of them actually turning to stone right in front of her.

Chapter VII

Caveat emptor

Back in the main atrium, Lucius and his bodyguards were long gone. Evening had arrived, things had calmed down again, and all was quiet and still, barring the occasional ominous rumble from Vesuvius. The Doctor and Caecilius were the only ones in the room now, and it was time to do some investigating.

The Doctor examined the hypocaust grille where Evelina had been breathing in the steam. He yanked the grille free, and stared down into the shaft, inspecting it with the sonic screwdriver.

Caecilius held up an oil lamp, unsure what the night had in store after the day's events. He didn't quite know why he trusted this man, but there was something in his face that he was drawn to, something entirely absent in Lucius's face: kindness. Even though he was very strange – and yes, a little bit scary – above all, he was kind, and here to help.

'Different sort of hypocaust,' mused the Doctor.

'Oh yes, we're very advanced in Pompeii,' said

Caecilius, with not inconsiderable pride in his city. 'In Rome, they're still using the old wood-burning furnaces, but we've got hot springs, leading right from Vesuvius itself.'

'Very clever. Who thought that up, then?

'The soothsayers, of course.'

'Of course they did, silly me. They think up everything around here.'

'We didn't always have this system. It was only constructed after the great earthquake, 17 years ago. An awful lot of damage. But we rebuilt.'

'Didn't you think of moving away?' asked the Doctor.

'Why? Once they were given the gift of sight, all the soothsayers could see that it was safe again. No chance of any more serious earthquakes happening now. There's the odd rumble here and there, yes, but nothing we can't manage. If there was going to be another big one, they'd have seen it. Everything's going to be just fine.'

The sound of grinding rocks came from below, churning and crunching. The Doctor looked down into the hypocaust again, frowning. 'The odd rumble, eh? What was that noise?'

'Happens all the time. They say the gods of the underworld are stirring.' Caecilius didn't seem concerned.

The Doctor tried to piece some of it together. 'So,

hang on, after the earthquake, is that when the sooth-sayers all started making sense?'

'Oh yes,' said Caecilius. 'Very much so. I mean, they'd always been, shall we say, imprecise? But after that, all of a sudden, the soothsayers, the augurs, the haruspex, all of them, they saw the truth, again and again. It's quite amazing. They can predict crops and rainfall with absolute precision.'

The Doctor frowned, being careful with his words. 'And they haven't said anything about tomorrow? Nothing at all?'

'No. Why, should they?'

'No reason, just asking,' said the Doctor. A thought struck him. 'But the soothsayers, not just Evelina, they all consume the vapours too, yes?'

'Yes. That's how they strengthen their abilities. I don't understand it, of course, but then I don't have their gift.'

The Doctor took the lamp and held it up to the steam. Specks of dust floated in the hot air. He let some of it touch his hand, and rubbed it between his fingers. The dust was solid. It was very light and fine, but he was able to pull it right out of the steam and touch it.

'Tiny particles of rock,' said the Doctor, surprised. 'They're breathing in Vesuvius.'

Caecilius was shocked. 'My daughter is breathing in bits of mountain? Well, that's the end of that. I don't care who she's promised to, or what it does to our status. This isn't right. She's not well, you can see she's not.'

'I'm sure she'll be fine. Just keep giving her lots of water, and—'

THUD! Something hit the roof, loudly, making them both jump. Another THUD. Then another. Metella called out from the other room, and ran in, just as something fell through the open atrium and into the water with a loud splash.

It was a dead bird.

Splash! Another one fell into the water, then several more, some hitting the roof, some landing in the room.

It was raining dead birds.

'Why are they drowning themselves?' shouted Metella over the noise.

The Doctor managed to catch one before it hit the water. It just lay in his hand lifelessly. 'They're not,' he said. 'They're already dead. They're just . . . falling out of the sky.'

The birds kept thundering down onto the roof and into the water. Then, as suddenly as it had started, it stopped.

Donna came running in, breathlessly. 'Oi! It's raining birds in the other room – oh.'

The Doctor looked out of the window. There were lots of birds lying in the street, and even more covering the next few houses. 'Localised shower of birds,' he said. 'Bet the soothsayers didn't soothsay that one.'

Caecilius led Metella away, comforting her, but in reality looking to be comforted himself.

Donna came over to join the Doctor at the window. 'There's a 17-year-old girl in there, whose arm is turning to stone. Everyone's psychic, except where the volcano is concerned. Some bloke who wouldn't understand a TV remote somehow knows all about us and electronic circuit boards. And now it's raining birds. What is going on?'

'Wait, what? Evelina's arm is turning to stone?'

'Looks like it to me.'

'Must be a side effect,' said the Doctor. 'She's been breathing in the stone dust from Vesuvius, but I suspect that's all over and done with now I've told them.'

'Good. She's a nice kid, she doesn't need that. What about the birds?'

'During the eruption, between pyroclastic surges, there was a wave of poisonous gas. Well, there was, or will be, from our current position in time, even though it's already happened, if we're being precise then technically the temporal tense is "had will have been", so from the relative position of—'

Donna shook her head. 'Gibberish. Talking gibberish. Again.'

'Sorry, that's the trouble with time travel, the grammar is a nightmare. That, and trying not to bump into yourself, which is more of an issue for me. Anyway, the

77

poison gas asphyxiated anyone it hit, they couldn't even smell it and then they were gone. These poor creatures must have flown right into a massive cloud of it.'

'But Vesuvius hasn't erupted yet.'

'I know, the timing's all wrong.'

Donna tried not to panic. If the timing was all wrong, then that meant they were in even more danger than they thought. 'We've still got until tomorrow, though, right? We're safe until then?'

Even the Doctor didn't look sure on this point. 'I don't know any more. Someone's interfering. Maybe it'll never go off. Maybe it'll go off at any moment.'

'OK, great,' said Donna, rolling her eyes. 'Remind me not to ask you anything ever again.'

'The bigger point is,' said the Doctor, 'Evelina and Lucius's duelling soothsayer show proved that they really do have the gift of seeing the future. If all the others are like that too, able to make accurate predictions, in exact detail, why is it that not a single one of them can see the massive volcanic eruption coming tomorrow? Surely that would be easier to see than crop harvests and rain showers. Someone's messing about with the natural order of things.'

'And that's *your* job,' said Donna, mostly with a straight face.

'That's right,' said the Doctor, before realising she was being sarcastic. He made a face at her.

'So we're staying?' Donna asked.

'We're staying. There's a mystery to solve here. Shenanigans are most definitely afoot.'

'Who d'you think you are now, Sherlock Holmes?'

'Taught him everything he knows,' said the Doctor airily.

Donna stared at him. She had to ask, even though asking the Doctor anything probably meant going down yet another rabbit hole of nonsense and overly long sentences. 'You mean, Arthur Conan Doyle? You taught Arthur Conan Doyle everything he knows?'

'No, Sherlock Holmes. They're two very different people.'

'Sher – I can't believe I'm actually having to say this – Sherlock Holmes isn't real.'

'Well, don't tell him that.'

'Oh my God, of COURSE he's not real!'

'Fictionalised, of course, so he could keep a low profile. One of his greatest tricks, making the world think he was just a story. "Just" a story! Stories can be more powerful than anything. If he hadn't pretended he wasn't real, he probably wouldn't be quite so celebrated. Conan Doyle published the stories, embellished quite a bit, they both pretended he'd made him up.'

'Right, OK, let's pretend that this isn't a load of nonsense, so how come nobody has ever mentioned this, ever?'

'Well of course Conan Doyle kept it quiet – he didn't share the royalties. Sherlock was furious.'

Donna pinched her temples. This was giving her a headache, as expected. She supposed it was her own fault for asking. 'This . . . this is a ridiculous conversation, and I'm not gonna continue to be part of it.'

'Probably wise,' said the Doctor. 'Oh, hang on, I can't wear my detective hat, Romana threw it away years ago. Probably wouldn't fit me now anyway, not with this head.'

'You'll just have to cope, somehow.'

The Doctor turned away from the window, with a renewed purpose. He marched back into the middle of the room, and found Quintus lazing around on a couch with some grapes. 'Quintus, me old son! This Lucius Petrus Dextrus bloke. Where does he live?'

'Nothing to do with me,' yawned Quintus. 'Today is a minimum effort day for me, and I intend to keep it going that way right through to the evening.'

'Let me try again. This Lucius Petrus Dextrus,' said the Doctor, producing a coin seemingly from behind Quintus's ear. 'Where does he live?'

Quintus's eyes widened when he saw the coin. 'I can show you,' he said. 'In fact, I can take you there. Whatever you need. Maybe we can stop off along the way for a quick livener.'

'Just take me to his house,' said the Doctor.

'Are you going to cause trouble?' asked Donna.

'Always.'

'What a surprise. I'll go check on Evelina, make sure she's OK. Don't get in any fights without me.'

Waving a flaming torch ahead of him, Quintus led the Doctor through the dark streets. The markets were closed now, everything packed away for tomorrow. Vesuvius loomed in the distance. As they approached a large, expensive-looking villa, Quintus pointed at it nervously.

'Lucius lives there. Don't tell my dad.'

'Only if you don't tell mine,' replied the Doctor. 'Come on. Give me a leg up, then pass me the torch.'

'You're going in?'

'No. *We're* going in.'

'Oh no,' said Quintus.

'Oh yes!'

Quintus wasn't sure, but figured that if this weird stranger was willing to hand money over so easily, there might be more coins coming along soon. It was worth the risk, if they were quick.

The Doctor and Quintus climbed in through the window of Lucius's villa. They were in a small study, with a desk covered in scrolls and reference materials. In the centre of the room, a hypocaust grille glowed brightly, even hotter and more intense than the ones in Caecilius's villa. The Doctor searched the room, while Quintus fidgeted, worried about being discovered.

'What are we looking for?' asked Quintus. 'And can we do it more quickly?'

'Just a feeling,' said the Doctor. 'If he's being given instructions, I want to know who is behind it, and why. Hello, what have we here . . .'

One wall had a large curtain draped over something hidden. The Doctor pulled it aside, and whistled.

There were six squares of marble, just like the one Caecilius had made.

'Well, well, well,' said the Doctor. 'Looks like "the rain and mist and wind" have been very busy.'

'The liar!' said Quintus, staring at the marble, surprised. 'He told my father it was the only one!'

'Plenty of marble merchants around here. Tell them all the same thing, get the components from different places, so no one can see what you're building. But why keep it a secret when nobody even knows what a circuit is yet? And what exactly *are* you building . . . ?'

'The future,' said Lucius, who had just walked into the room behind them, accompanied by two very large, armed guards. 'We are building the future. As dictated by the gods.'

The guards brandished their swords. The Doctor and Quintus were trapped.

Chapter VIII

Dies irae

Evelina was sitting up in her bedroom, feeling a bit better. She had colour in her cheeks, and there was no trace of the strange vision that had put her into a trancelike state earlier. She'd forgotten most of what she had said, she just knew it had probably come across as quite rude. It was embarrassing, but she couldn't help it: when the visions came, they gripped her tightly, and she had to get them out of her head. It had been like that ever since she first received the gift. Transfixed by images and sounds flowing through her, she was simply the vessel for the visions. For the gods.

Having a higher purpose didn't make it hurt any less. The headaches were getting worse, her memory was hazy, and she couldn't even bear to look at whatever was happening to her arm. The gods must know what they were doing, even if she didn't.

Sometimes she wished she could just have a normal life again, like the childhood friends she'd left behind. She saw them occasionally, in passing. Once, they had all been close, laughing together, not a care in the world, but now they went quiet as she walked by. They were scared of her, of who she had become, of who she *would* become. She'd left all that normality behind, and she missed it so much. But she wanted to do her family proud, even more so than pleasing the gods. If this helped her mother, father and brother all gain status and stay safe, then it was a duty she was happy to perform.

Moments like this though, it was easy to forget about that, and pretend to be normal again. The strange visitor called Donna had come to see her and, after copious apologies from Evelina, they just talked and laughed like ordinary people.

Donna was trying on a purple outfit, and doing a variety of exaggerated poses. One particularly over-the-top pose made Evelina burst out laughing.

Donna looked mock-offended. 'You're not supposed to laugh!' she said. 'Thanks for that. What do you think? The goddess Venus . . .' She posed again, flinging her arms out wide.

'Oh, that's sacrilege,' said Evelina, but she was more amused than shocked. Surely any gods worth their salt wouldn't mind people having a bit of fun, as long as it didn't hurt anyone else.

'Nice to see you laughing, though,' said Donna.

Evelina smiled. She couldn't actually remember the last time she had laughed like this, properly laughed so much that her cheeks ached. It was a lovely feeling. Donna was very funny. She had a natural gift for making you feel good about yourself . . . and for silly voices.

'You do look lovely,' said Evelina. 'It suits you well. I love your hair. It's like the evening sunlight across the river.'

Donna smiled, and Evelina saw that hint of sadness in her face again. It had been there ever since she arrived, and Evelina couldn't figure it out. How could someone so warm and funny have such a weight on their shoulders? Maybe it was the things Lucius had said to her; he did have that effect on people. But no, this was something else. Donna looked haunted by something, as if she was desperate to talk about it but kept stopping herself. Evelina didn't need to be psychic to see that.

'So,' said Donna. 'What do you do round here, in old Pompeii, girls your age? Have you got mates? Do you go hanging about round the shops? TK Maxximus?'

Evelina grew sombre again, reminded of the path she was on now, and the one she had left behind. It had been nice pretending for a while, but there was no getting away from it. 'I am promised to the Sisterhood for the rest of my life.'

'Do you get a choice in that?'

'It's not my decision. The Sisters chose for me. I have the gift of sight.'

Donna spoke very carefully and delicately, clearly still avoiding what she really wanted to say. 'Right, so . . . what can you see happening tomorrow?'

'Is tomorrow special?'

'You tell me. What do you see?

Evelina closed her eyes, and concentrated. She furrowed her brow. This wasn't a vision, not like the deep, strong ones she would occasionally get. This was merely a deliberate glance at the near future, one that she could control. The gift took many forms. If she concentrated, she could see just a short way ahead down the road, to the end of the next day or thereabouts. It didn't tax her as much as the bigger visions, those would come upon her whether she chose to have them or not. She looked ahead now, and saw . . . a normal day.

She opened her eyes again, shrugging. 'The sun will rise, the sun will set. Nothing special at all.' She smiled at Donna. Maybe that was what had been worrying her this whole time? Maybe she was scared that something bad would happen to her tomorrow. Now that Evelina had looked ahead, she was happy to put her mind at rest, and let her know that everything would be fine.

But it didn't seem to lift Donna's spirits, quite the opposite. She sat there, biting her lip for a minute. Evelina felt bad for her, and wished she could help.

'What is it?' she asked. 'What are you so worried about? What does tomorrow mean to you?'

'Look,' said Donna. 'Don't tell the Doctor I said anything, he'll kill me . . . but I've sort of got a prophecy too.'

Evelina gasped in shock. 'There is only one true voice of prophecy,' she said, scared. 'You are not permitted!'

'But everything I'm about to say is true, I swear,' said Donna. Evelina shook her head, upset, but Donna continued. 'Just listen. Tomorrow, that mountain, Vesuvius, is going to explode. It's going to fill the air with ash and rocks, tons and tons of it, and this whole town is going to get buried.'

'No! That's not true!'

'It is. I wish it wasn't, but it is. You have to believe me. I'm trying to help you.'

Evelina couldn't bear to hear it. 'Please, stop this,' she said, trying her best to prevent her friend from getting into more trouble. She had seen what the authorities did, in the name of the gods, to people who interfered. She had no desire to see Donna hurt.

'I'm sorry,' said Donna. 'I'm really sorry. Everyone's going to die, unless you leave now. Look, even if you don't believe me, just tell your family to get out of town. Just for one day, just for tomorrow, have a little day trip away somewhere. But you have got to get out. You have to leave Pompeii.'

'This is a false prophecy,' gasped Evelina. She covered her eyes with her palms, displaying the eyes on the back of her hands. She formed a psychic link with the Sisters in the temple – she needed to speak with them immediately. Connecting minds was one of the first things she had learned how to do, even before the visions started, and she found it as easy as talking to someone in the same room.

'Evelina?' persisted Donna, not realising she could now be seen and heard by the Sisters. 'I'm sorry, but you've got to hear me out. Just listen to me. Can you hear me?'

Evelina shook her head, keeping her hands over her eyes. If she didn't inform the Sisters, then anything might happen to her and to her family. 'Sisters,' she said. 'A new prophecy. The fall of Pompeii.' She could see everything that was happening in the Temple of Sibyl now. She could see Spurrina and the others listening to the conversation, and heard what they said, the words echoing and drifting as if travelling underwater. They all continued speaking inside their minds, sitting silently. Until a decision was made.

When Evelina heard the response, she yanked her hands away from her eyes, breaking the psychic connection. She fell back onto her bed, like a puppet whose strings had been cut. The conversation had weakened her, partly because of the effort required to make the psychic connection, partly because of the outcome.

'Evelina?' said Donna. 'Are you OK? What happened?

Who were you talking to just then? What was happening? Evelina!'

Evelina couldn't explain, she was too exhausted. Besides, there was nothing either of them could do about it now. The Sisters had their orders. They would be coming for Donna soon. If Evelina tried to stop them, she would suffer the same fate. They were coming for Donna.

They were going to kill her.

Chapter IX

Tempus fugit

In Lucius's villa, despite the piping hot steam from the hypocaust, the atmosphere was decidedly frosty. It was bad enough that the Doctor and Quintus had been discovered breaking in, but they had also found the strange marble squares alongside the one Caecilius had constructed. Lucius was keeping secrets, and he did not look like the sort of man who would let them leave to tell the tale.

Quintus felt queasy, nervous at what might happen now. He'd never been in trouble before, not real trouble. Sure, there had been plenty of late nights, hanging around with friends, laughing, accidentally breaking things, singing too loudly, 'borrowing' street signs and falling into fountains. Nothing that teenagers hadn't done since the invention of spare time. At the end of the summer, he'd have to think about his further education but, for now, evenings and weekends were for having fun.

The party was definitely over in this room, though.

Quintus was worried for himself mainly, of course, but he was even more concerned for his family. Lucius was a powerful, dangerous man. There were more than a few rumours of people who had crossed him ending up in the foundations of new buildings. Some even claimed you could make out the shape of his ex-business partner in the outside wall of the villa and that, every time Lucius entered or left the building, he would pat the wall to greet him and laugh. This could mean very bad news for Quintus's family.

Lucius glared. The soldiers stood watch, candlelight glinting off their sharp swords. But the Doctor seemed oblivious, happily diving into the awkward situation as if it was just a tiny misunderstanding. Quintus was fascinated at how casual he was; he'd never met anyone quite like him. Surely he must have some reason to be so confident, some sort of skills or secret knowledge? Nobody could just breeze through life like that otherwise.

Maybe he was just weird and lucky – or possibly unlucky, depending on how this went. Quintus guessed that he'd find out either way very soon.

'Well, let's have a looksee,' said the Doctor, examining the marble squares. He grabbed one, swapped it around with another, switched another two, turned one upside down, and another sideways. 'Put this one here, that one there, keep that one this way around, bish bash bosh, and what have you got?'

Lucius stared. 'Enlighten me.'

'Oh, the soothsayer doesn't know something?'

'The seed may float on the breeze in any direction,' sneered Lucius.

'Yeah, I knew you were going to say that,' said the Doctor.

Quintus was amazed. He'd never seen Lucius so unsure of himself; the man was clearly bluffing. How could that be, when he had the gift of sight? There was something going on here. Perhaps he wasn't the great seer he claimed to be.

The Doctor was still talking cheerfully. 'Anyway, for your information, this particular circuit is an energy converter.'

'An energy converter of what?'

The Doctor shrugged happily. 'I don't know. Isn't that brilliant? I love not knowing! Keeps me on my toes. It must be awful being a prophet, waking up every morning, is it raining, yes it is, I said so . . . Takes all the fun out of life. No surprises. But who designed this, Lucius, eh? Not you, you don't even know what it is. Who gave you these instructions? What do they want?'

Lucius's face grew more and more red as the Doctor kept talking, until he started to look like an angry tomato. Finally, he couldn't take it any more. 'You insult the gods. There can be only one sentence. At arms!'

The soldiers drew their swords.

'Oh, *morituri te salutant*,' said the Doctor.

'Celtic prayers won't help you now,' said Lucius.

This was it, thought Quintus. He was about to perish, in this room, away from his family, with his whole life still ahead of him. It wasn't fair. He had so many things left that he wanted to do. Places he wanted to see. People he wanted to kiss. Food he wanted to taste. And he'd been working up the courage to ask his friend Titus if he wanted to go out on a date, he'd seen the way he looked at him and now regretted every time he'd chickened out of saying something. Why had he let himself get drawn into this situation, with this odd person he'd only just met? There was only one possible way out: begging.

'It was him, sir,' Quintus pleaded, pointing at the Doctor. 'He made me do it, I didn't even want to be here. Mr Dextrus, please, don't!'

'Come on now, Quintus, dignity in death,' said the Doctor. He didn't seem angry, more disappointed. Quintus immediately felt bad. He straightened up a bit, and tried to act brave, even if he wasn't feeling it.

'Shame, though,' said the Doctor. 'We haven't even made our funeral arrangements. I want flowers, lots of flowers, big, brightly coloured flowers. And music, very loud music. And dancing, lots of dancing, *terrible* dancing, I don't want any good dancing, just people having fun. And food, there's never enough food—'

'Silence!' barked Lucius.

The Doctor stepped forward. 'Lucius, I respect your victory. Shake on it? Come on. Dying man's wish?'

The Doctor held his hand out, but Lucius didn't move. The Doctor darted forward quickly, grabbing the man's right hand. He grinned at the panic that suddenly appeared on Lucius's face. Then yanked, hard.

There was an awful, loud *crack*.

Lucius's forearm had snapped off. The Doctor was holding a stone right arm, as if he'd just taken it from a statue. Quintus stared in shock. What was going on? The Doctor didn't seem surprised at all, which made things even stranger.

Even the soldiers were taken aback. This was news to them, too. But Lucius was unabashed. He actually seemed proud.

'Show me,' said the Doctor. 'Honestly, I'm on your side, I can help.'

Lucius threw back his cloak, showing that the whole of his arm had turned to stone, along with part of his shoulder. 'The work of the gods,' he said.

"He's made of stone,' said Quintus, horrified. What was this nightmare? A man turning into a statue? Still, the Doctor didn't seem startled, as if he had had his suspicions confirmed. How could he know that?

'Armless enough, though,' said the Doctor. 'Sorry, couldn't resist. Watch out!'

The Doctor threw the arm to Lucius, who wasn't

quick enough to catch it. The arm shattered on the ground. The soldiers began to attack, but the Doctor pulled a strange device out of his pocket and aimed it at the plinth, which started to vibrate. The marble squares all wobbled and toppled over.

'The carvings!' yelled Lucius, and the soldiers scrambled to catch them before they hit the ground. In the chaos, Doctor and Quintus scrambled back out of the window.

As Quintus threw a terrified glance over his shoulder, he saw that Lucius wasn't following. Instead, he ran to the hypocaust grille, and called down into it. 'Lord of the mountain, I beseech you. This man would prevent the rise of Pompeii. Lord, I beg of you. Show yourself. Show yourself!'

Flames roared under the grille, lighting up Lucius's impassioned face, and Quintus turned away to run before anything else happened.

Out in the street, the Doctor and Quintus slowed down when it became clear nobody was giving chase. Quintus was relieved, but slightly uneasy about what Lucius had been saying into the hypocaust. An appeal to the gods? He and the Doctor had committed several crimes tonight, it wouldn't be unexpected. But Lucius wasn't entirely innocent either.

'Doctor, his arm,' said Quintus, trying to make sense of it all. 'Is that what's happening to Evelina?'

'It's only just started for her,' said the Doctor. 'But don't worry, I have a feeling your mum and dad will put a stop to all that.'

'Well if they won't, I will. I don't want her turning into . . . into that, whatever it is. I don't want her being like him.'

'No chance of that, trust me. We just need to work out what's going on. Come on, I think we—'

The street rumbled slightly. They stopped, and listened.

'Is that the mountain again?' asked Quintus.

There was another rumble. Louder this time. More of an echoing thud. Even the Doctor finally looked a little bit on edge this time, which worried Quintus. If he hadn't been scared in Lucius's villa, what could possibly scare him now?

'No,' said the Doctor. 'It's closer than that. Almost like—'

Whump. Whump. Whump. Whump.

'Footsteps . . . Underground footsteps.'

The whumping sound got closer. The street shook with each one and, as the sounds got closer, things started falling down, knocked over by the vibrations. A sign. A display stand. A cart. The grille on an outdoor hypocaust suddenly blew upwards like a geyser.

Then there were more footsteps. Getting closer. Faster.

'Run!' yelled the Doctor, grabbing Quintus's hand.

They ran off together. Normally, Quintus would feel a bit odd letting a grown adult stranger grab his hand to run, but it felt perfectly natural for some reason. It wasn't the weirdest thing that had happened today, that was for certain.

Quintus and the Doctor ran into the family villa, where everyone was already assembled in the main atrium, confused by the strange new noises. Quintus was relieved to see that they were all OK. For now.

'What is that noise?' said Metella. 'Doesn't sound like Vesuvius.'

'It's not,' said the Doctor. 'We're being followed. Everybody, get out of here, now!'

'Have you broken something?' asked Donna. 'I told you not to go breaking anything without me.'

The whumping sounds reached the villa, and started coming from the ground right underneath them.

One of the hypocaust grilles in the room blew upwards in a frenzy of steam. The heavy grille clanged on the floor, tossed aside as if it barely weighed anything.

Steam kept pouring out of the hypocaust, shaking it violently, as the whumping sounds got louder. Everybody crowded away from it, as the ground started cracking around it. Something big was trying to get out. Something very big. Far too big for the small opening.

The Doctor sprang into action, running over and squinting to try and see what was inside the hypocaust. 'Who are you?' he shouted. He frowned. 'What is that? Is that a Krarg? No, it can't be. It's something worse.'

'What's going on?' asked Caecilius.

Then the Doctor saw something happening in the hypocaust that made him leap back away from it. He turned to the others, urgently. 'Get some water. Quintus, all of you, get water, quick!'

Quintus ran to the corridor entrance, and shouted to the Major Domo. 'Buckets! Lots of buckets, bring them all in here! Now!' He looked back into the room just in time to see what happened next.

The ground buckled, shook and sank in on itself slightly. Then, in an explosion of rocks and dust, it burst upwards, as something like an enormous burning rock climbed out.

The creature was eight or nine feet tall, nearly touching the ceiling. It was made of splintered stone with a fiery core, like a living furnace. On top of its head, there was a thick crest which looked a lot like a Roman soldier's helmet. The fire in its eyes, nose and mouth burned brightly, angrily.

'The gods are with us,' said Evelina. She looked like she recognised the creature, as if she had been expecting its arrival somehow.

Everybody kept well back, except for the Major Domo of the house, who stepped forward, entranced by the creature. He raised his hands in supplication, reverently. 'Blessed are we to see the gods!'

The fire creature looked down at him, and instantly blasted fire from its mouth like a burning fountain, engulfing the unfortunate man in flames. He was incinerated in seconds, the fire so hot it left nothing but ash. His screams echoed briefly after he was vaporised. Then he was gone, like he was never there.

The Doctor kept a safe distance, but tried to communicate. 'Talk to me! That's all I want! Talk to me. Just tell me who you are. Don't hurt these people.'

Quintus waved more people in when they arrived with buckets, and he started directing them to the pool at the centre of the atrium, grabbing a bucket himself. 'Fill these up, now,' he told them.

The Doctor was still trying to reason with the fire creature. 'Talk to me,' he yelled. 'I'm the Doctor! Just tell me who you are.'

But the creature wasn't here to talk. It was here to burn. It turned towards the Doctor, and its eyes and mouth glowed bright with fire, getting ready to shoot out flame again.

Quintus and the others dunked the buckets into the water. It was controlled chaos, but they swiftly got the buckets filled and ran over. They lined themselves up, got the timing right, and all threw their buckets at the same moment. The water drenched the creature, hissing loudly as it hit the incredibly hot surface. The fire dimmed slightly as the water steamed, and the heat started to dissipate. The creature looked stricken, and then there was a domino effect as the rest of its body cooled slightly. Within seconds, the creature started crumbling into rocks, until it collapsed into a pile of smoking pebbles and gravel on the floor. The fire was out.

Nobody moved for a moment.

'At the risk of stating the obvious,' said Caecilius, 'that was terrifying. Poor Rhombus, it just … it just murdered him. What is happening?'

Quintus spoke up, knowing it would get him into trouble, but he wanted to help. 'I saw Lucius calling out to someone when we were leaving. Shouting down into the hypocaust. I think he sent that thing after us.'

Metella was shocked. 'Lucius did this?'

'He's been lying to us,' said Quintus. 'He had lots of those marble square things made by other people, and his arm has turned to stone. But what was it? Doctor, have you seen anything like this before?'

'Carapace of stone, held together by internal magma,' said the Doctor, poking through the rubble, sniffing a handful of hot gravel. 'Stinks of sulphur. Living, molten rock. They feed off the heat from the mountain, when they wander too far from the source, a bit of water tips the balance, causes a chain reaction. Not too difficult to stop. But I reckon that's just a foot soldier.'

'Good, OK, right, I see,' said Caecilius. 'Now, can anyone explain what any of that meant?'

And then the bizarre, unearthly sound filled the air again, the weird foghorn that seemed to echo inside their heads. It was even louder this time, the noise shaking small rocks loose. Gradually, it died away.

'We've been hearing that a lot,' said Quintus. 'The mountain has only started doing it recently. What could it mean?'

'It means that someone's messing around with things they don't understand,' said the Doctor. 'Or worse, they do understand, but they're doing it anyway. Sounds like the rocks are grinding against each other. Massive stresses and strains. Forces of incredible power.'

Metella glared at him. 'Doctor, or whatever your name is, you bring bad luck to this house.'

'I thought your son was brilliant, aren't you going to thank him?' said the Doctor.

'Come here,' said Metella, folding Quintus into a hug, relieved to have him home safe. He hugged her back, surprised but grateful. Maybe he wasn't in trouble after all. Maybe things were going to be all right.

'Still,' said the Doctor. 'Whatever these things are, if there are aliens involved, it's a good job we stayed, isn't it Donna? Donna? This is the quietest you've ever been, what's the matter?'

He looked all around the room.

But Donna was gone.

Chapter X

Rigor mortis

'Did anyone see where Donna went?' said the Doctor.

Evelina looked upset. She nodded at the Doctor, and he ran over to her.

'What happened?' he said.

'They've taken her,' whispered Evelina, trembling.

'Taken her? Who?' barked the Doctor.

'The Sisters. It was when we were gathering the buckets, I saw them in the other room. They were all here. They took her while we were occupied with the beast of fire.'

'Why didn't you say anything?'

'There was no time, it all happened so fast. I'm sorry, it's all my fault. I told them about her false prophecy, they would never have known otherwise. I didn't think any of this would happen. She was my friend, and I betrayed her, but they still did this to us. Why would they send a monster to our home? I am promised to them!'

It went against her every instinct to betray the

Sisterhood. But this felt wrong, all wrong. Sending giant mountain creatures to put her family in danger, kill the Major Domo, who had always been kind to her, and now kidnap her new friend – none of this was in the prophecy. None of this was their purpose.

The Doctor looked at her and softened his voice.

'It's OK,' he said. 'I don't blame you. The Sisters have been manipulating you, all of you. All of Pompeii, by the sound of it. What do you mean, Donna's false prophecy?'

'She told me that everyone would die here tomorrow. That the mountain would kill us all. She was wrong, but I had to tell the others.'

The Doctor looked exasperated, but not surprised. Evelina realised that he already knew about this, and now she was more frightened than ever. If these strange visitors both believed that everyone here was about to die, maybe she needed to take it seriously.

'Don't worry about that now,' said the Doctor. 'Just tell me where they've taken her, and I can fix this. I'm here to help.'

'The temple,' said Evelina, afraid for him, for them all. 'They've taken her to the temple.'

In the Temple of Sibyl, Donna was not in a good mood. It was fair to say this was probably the worst mood she'd been in all year.

And she'd had a pretty spectacularly bad few

months, even before reconnecting with the Doctor. In any other year, being hunted down by a lunatic alien nanny and lumps of living fat would have been the worst thing ever – but this year, that barely scraped the top five. There was the disastrous night out chasing a taxi driver she thought was an alien in disguise, which resulted in her online taxi app somehow dropping her passenger rating to below zero. That was quite an achievement; the company actually sent her a certificate. Cancelled her account, of course, but they were still impressed. Then there was the Bad Haircut Incident of February, which her friends and family were ordered to NEVER mention again, even though it had grown out since and she had deleted all photos of the offending barnet. And then there was the speed-dating evening her mum had forced her to go on, during which she had slapped three men, punched two, and been barred from an entire street. And those were just the top three bad things to happen. There were so many others she wished she could forget, too, including the event everyone simply referred to in hushed tones as KebabGate.

But none of them had ended with her tied to a sacrificial altar, in a creepy secret temple, with some sort of spooky druids standing around chanting and waving knives. So this pipped them all to the top spot. By some considerable distance. She just hoped she would live to tell the tale.

Spurrina and the other Sisters stood around the altar in a circle, together with the Soothsayer. Spurrina took out an enormous, curved dagger, inscribed with ancient lettering. Donna caught a glimpse of it, and her eyes widened.

'You have got to be kidding me,' said Donna.

'The false prophet will surrender both her blood, and her breath,' chanted Spurrina.

'I'll surrender you in a minute,' yelled Donna. 'Don't you DARE!'

'You will be silent!' shouted Thalina, imperiously.

'Listen, sister,' Donna yelled back even louder, who wasn't about to be out-shouted, especially not by some weirdo in a smock. 'You might have eyes on the back of your hands, but you'll have eyes in the back of your head by the time I've finished with you. Let! Me! Go!'

It was no use. As the other Sisters kept chanting, Spurrina lifted the sacrificial dagger high into the air. Candlelight glinted off it. Donna flung herself around, trying to wriggle out of the ropes, but it was no use.

'This prattling voice will cease for ever,' said Spurrina.

'Oh, that'll be the day,' said the Doctor, breezing into the room, as if nothing strange was going on. The Sisters stared at him in shock. One even covered her eyes, but then realised her hand-eyes could still see him, and quickly shuffled around trying to cover those ones too.

'No man is allowed to enter the Temple of Sibyl,' said Spurrina, scandalised.

'Oh, that's all right, it's just us girls,' grinned the Doctor, wandering around. 'Y'know, I met the Sibyl once. Yeah. Hell of a woman. Blimey, she could dance the tarantella. Nice teeth. Truth be told, I think she had a bit of a thing for me. I said, it'd never last, she said, I know. Well, she would. You all right there, Donna?'

Donna glanced at the ropes, incredulous. This called for some heavy sarcasm. 'Oh, yeah, great, never better.'

'I like the toga.'

'Thanks, yeah. Really goes well with these ropes, I thought.'

'Hmm, not so much,' said the Doctor. He whipped out the sonic screwdriver, aimed, and the vibrations loosened the ropes enough for Donna to pull herself free. The Sisters backed away, scared of this new development. The interloper clearly had some powers.

'What magic is this?' said Spurrina.

'Let me tell you about the Sibyl,' said the Doctor. 'The founder of this religion. She'd be ashamed of you. All her wisdom and insight turned sour. Is that how you spread the word, eh? On the blade of a knife?'

'Yes! A knife that now welcomes you,' said Spurrina, brandishing it. She started to lunge forwards.

But the scuffle was interrupted by the High Priestess, who sat up behind the curtains. 'Show me this man,' she said.

The Sisters prostrated themselves as they faced her. 'High Priestess!' said Spurrina. 'The stranger would defile us!'

'Let me see,' said the High Priestess, craning to see through the fabric. 'This one is different. He carries starlight in his wake.'

'Very perceptive,' said the Doctor, staring hard at the silhouette. 'Where do these words of wisdom come from?'

'The gods whisper to me.'

'They've done far more than that,' the Doctor said. 'Might I beg audience? Look upon the High Priestess?'

The silhouette waved a hand to the Sisters, granting permission. Reluctantly, Spurrina and Thalina pulled the curtain aside, revealing the figure behind the shape at last.

The High Priestess was almost entirely made of stone.

Evelina was just at the start of the process. The High Priestess was almost at the end. She looked like a rough plaster cast, but blackened from smoke and flame, half melted. Living stone, walking magma. Although not exactly walking, she could barely sit up. Her face was merely an approximation now, with dark holes for eyes, and a liquid charcoal mouth that moved with difficulty, like hot tar.

The Doctor and Donna stared at her, shocked.

'Oh my god,' said Donna, in horrified fascination. 'What's happened to you?'

'The Heavens have blessed me,' said the High Priestess. It was no idle claim, she clearly genuinely believed it was a blessing. It was difficult to tell, given how she looked, but she seemed to be smiling.

The Doctor pointed at her arm. 'If I might?'

She nodded, and held her arm out to him. He touched it, gently, feeling how solid it was, dust crumbling under his fingertips.

'Just like Evelina's arm,' said Donna.

'And Lucius, too,' said the Doctor. 'Does it hurt?'

'It is necessary,' said the High Priestess.

'Who told you that? Who said it was necessary?'

'The voices.'

'Is that what's going to happen to Evelina?' asked Donna. 'Wait, is this what's going to happen to all of you?'

'The blessings are manifold,' said Spurrina, stepping forward, pulling the robe back from her wrist. Her arm was turning to the same faded stone as Evelina and Lucius's arms. The other Sisters did the same. All of their arms had started the same process. But their eyes shone with holy fervour, excited to rise to the same level as the gods.

'They're stone. They're all stone,' said Donna.

'Exactly,' said the Doctor. 'The people of Pompeii are turning to stone *before* the volcano erupts. But why?'

'This word,' said the High Priestess, confused. 'This image in your mind. This . . . *volcano*. What is that?'

'More to the point,' said the Doctor, 'why don't you know about it? Who *are* you?'

'I am the High Priestess of the Sibylline, Mother of the—'

'No, no, no, I'm talking to the creature inside you, the thing that's seeding itself into a human body, in the dust, in the lungs, taking over the flesh and turning it into . . . what?'

'Your knowledge is impossible,' said the High Priestess. Or did she? It looked like someone else was speaking for her now, as if something had shifted inside her, in her mind. Something was gaining control. Speaking through her.

'Oh, but you can read my mind,' said the Doctor. 'You know it's not impossible. I demand you tell me who you are.'

'We . . . are . . . awakening . . .' said something through the High Priestess. Her voice was grating, becoming rougher, as the consciousness inside her gained in strength.

'The voice of the gods!' said Spurrina. She fell to her knees, as did the other Sisters, and they all began chanting.

'Words of wisdom, words of power . . . words of wisdom, words of power . . .' they chanted, over and over, as the High Priestess grew stronger and louder.

Steam rose up from her, as she continued to change right in front of them, the stone grinding as it became firmer, heat rising in the cracks.

'Name yourself!' shouted the Doctor, over the increasing noise. 'Planet of origin! Galactic coordinates! Species designation according to the Universal Ratification of the Shadow Proclamation!'

'We are rising,' said the High Priestess. 'Ascending.'

'Tell me your name!' yelled the Doctor.

The High Priestess drew herself up to her full height, steaming, fire starting to glow inside her. She opened her mouth, and *roared*.

'PYROVILE!'

Chapter XI

Carpe diem

The Doctor stared at the High Priestess – or at the creature that used to be her. She was a Pyrovile now.

The Sisters were now chanting 'Pyrovile' over and over, their eyes almost rolling back up into their heads, enraptured now that one of their gods was right here.

'Er . . . what's a Pyrovile?' asked Donna, who was rapidly starting to feel like the last normal person left on the planet.

'Well, that is,' said the Doctor. 'That's a Pyrovile. Growing inside her. She's at about the halfway stage, I'd say.'

'What, so she's turning into one of those gigantic things from the villa?'

'Yep. That was an adult Pyrovile.'

The High Priestess glared at them. 'And the breath of a Pyrovile will incinerate you, Doctor.' She stood up, fire building up in her chest, and gathering inside her mouth.

The Doctor stepped forward, unafraid, reaching

into his jacket. 'I must warn you,' he said, his face deathly serious. 'I'm armed.'

Donna hadn't known the Doctor for very long, not as long as his previous companions, certainly not as long as his many enemies. But one thing she knew, that everyone knew, was that his capacious pockets were filled with all kinds of weird and wonderful things. She didn't know how he fitted so much into them, without them bulging out sideways like old-fashioned, baggy jodhpurs, but somehow he managed it. He always had the right device for every occasion. Basically, if he was reaching into his pocket and looking stern, then you were in *big* trouble. Donna wondered what amazing device or weapon he was about to pull out now. Whatever it was, it was likely to be impressive and it would definitely save the day. She braced herself, ready to be dazzled. Somehow, the others in the room picked up on this, too. Maybe it was their psychic ability, maybe it was the ominous expression on his face. But they all knew, immediately, that he was about to reveal something extremely powerful.

Everyone froze, as the Doctor slowly pulled his hand out of his jacket, revealing his secret weapon.

It was a water pistol.

Not one of those big, pump-action, super-soaker types. That might have looked the part. No, it was a small, child's water pistol. Yellow, transparent plastic. With an orange tip.

Donna did a double take when she saw it. Then a triple take for good measure.

It couldn't have been any smaller or less threatening, but the Doctor wielded it like he was a hard-bitten cop on the streets of 1970s New York City, carrying a massive hand cannon.

Nobody moved.

Donna was pretty sure everyone was thinking the same thing she was. It didn't *look* like a dangerous weapon. It was clearly just a small, silly, yellow thing, and so obviously not a threat. But the Doctor was holding it with such supreme confidence, it was as if it could destroy them all with a careless trigger pull. It had to be real, surely? Donna didn't think even the Doctor would try a bluff that huge.

The Doctor jerked his head towards a nearby grille. 'Donna. Get that grille open.'

'What for?' said Donna, still taken aback by the yellow plastic water pistol. She couldn't take her eyes off it.

'Just open the thing!' The Doctor waggled his head, urging her to hurry up. He turned back to the creature inhabiting what was left of the High Priestess's body. 'What are the Pyrovile doing here?'

'We fell from the heavens,' said the creature. 'We fell so far and so fast, we were rendered into dust.'

'Right, aliens made of stone, shattered on impact. When was that?'

'We have slept beneath. For thousands of years.'

Donna kept working on the grille, as the Doctor slowly circled around, keeping the water pistol trained on the Pyrovile.

'OK,' he said, 'so the big earthquake 17 years ago woke you up, and now you're using human bodies to reconstitute yourselves. But why the psychic powers?'

'We opened their minds and found such gifts.'

'Fine, so you force yourself inside a human brain, use the latent psychic talent to bond, yeah, I get that. I get it. But seeing the future? That is way beyond psychic. You can see through time. Where does the gift of prophecy come from? And why can't this lot predict a volcano? Why is it being hidden?'

Donna finally yanked the grille open. 'Got it!' she yelled.

'Good. Get down,' said the Doctor.

Donna stared into the hole, unenthusiastically. 'What, down there?'

'Yes, down there!' He turned back to the Pyrovile. 'Tell me. All these psychic visions, why can't anybody see the volcano eruption?'

Spurrina was staring at him, trying to push through his mental barrier. Finally, she caught a glimpse of what she was looking for. She smiled. 'Sisters!' she shouted. 'I see into his mind. The weapon is harmless!'

The Doctor knew the game was up. Fair enough, it

116

had lasted longer than he expected, and given them enough time to find an escape route. He shrugged. 'Yeah,' he said. 'But it's got to sting . . .'

He squirted a few pathetic streams of water at the High Priestess. It sizzled on her rocky, flaky skin, and she recoiled in pain.

The Doctor ran over to the grille, where Donna was waiting. 'Get down there, I said!'

They both jumped in.

As the Doctor and Donna slid to a stop at the bottom of the incline, they could still hear the Pyrovile Priestess roaring in anger above them. They scrambled to their feet. Donna was impressed at the Doctor's sheer gall, and couldn't believe what he had just done.

'You just fought off one of those things,' she said, 'with a *water pistol*. I bloody love you!'

The Doctor winked, and spun the water pistol around his finger like an old Wild West gunslinger. 'Just a variation on the old clipboard trick,' he said. 'Carry a clipboard and act confident, you can walk past any security guard. Well, anywhere except the planet Ryman-IV: clipboards are banned there, apparently, they look rude. Takes all sorts, eh? Come on, down this way.'

'Where are we going?'

'Into the volcano.'

'Into the – oh, no, that's a big volca-nope. No way.'

'Yes way. *Appian* Way!'

Donna would have told him off for the pun, but flames roared down from the grille opening above, and they had to run to avoid being singed.

They kept going, deeper into the volcano.

Chapter XII

Alea iacta est

The Sisters continued to chant, as the Pyrovile Priestess raged, her shouts echoing through the temple. She was still too weak and newly formed to chase the intruders, but she didn't need to. They had gone into the mountain. They would not come back out. The others of her kind would soon make sure of that. The newcomers could not be allowed to jeopardise the Pyrovile plans. Not after the long ages of waiting.

She drew herself up to her full, considerable height, and formed a psychic link with Lucius.

'The stranger would threaten our great endeavour,' she said to him, from her mind to his mind. 'The time has come. The prophecy must advance.'

Lucius received the instructions and spoke the words along with her, sitting by the steam from the hypocaust in his villa, dazed as the words landed directly in his mind.

'The prophecy must advance,' he muttered. 'Thy will be done.'

He snapped out of his trance, and called out to his personal guard soldiers.

'We must go to the mountain. Vesuvius awaits.'

He sat down to rest while the soldiers assembled and made the arrangements. The stone infection had spread further, growing more quickly. It had moved past his shoulder, into the side of his chest, and was encroaching on his neck too, making it difficult to breathe and speak. Once the transformation was fully complete, it would be easier; he would even be able to regrow an arm. But this halfway stage was trickier to negotiate. When it reached his legs, he would be temporarily unable to walk. The work had to be completed while he was still mobile. The gods demanded it.

Lucius had a strong sense of responsibility, particularly to the gods. He had never been a kind man, which made it easier to carry out his duty. He was always ready to do what was necessary, no matter who got hurt or killed in the process. It was all for the greater good. These new gods delivered on their promises, unlike every other authority figure in his life. The military had let him down. His father had been a hard taskmaster who ultimately proved to be unreliable. Nobody had been consistent. Now that Lucius had found new masters to serve, masters who did what they said and rewarded obedience, he had seized his role with enthusiasm. The prophecy was almost complete, and soon he would become a god himself.

The two soldiers came back, saluting. They were ready. Vesuvius was several miles away, so they would need fresh horses. In the other room, more soldiers gathered together, talking quietly amongst themselves. It was time.

Lucius stood up stiffly. Today was going to be a good day. A victorious day. He could feel it.

Outside Vesuvius, at a cave entrance to the mountain, Lucius approached, leading half a dozen soldiers, each carrying one of the marble squares. His two personal guard soldiers stood watching nearby, but there was nobody else in the vicinity. The sun was just below the horizon, filling the air with a sense of impending opportunity. Lucius walked to the front of the cave, and called out to his masters.

'Oh mighty Vesuvius! Accept these offerings, in Vulcan's design. Show unto us, I beseech you, the gods of the Underworld!'

With a mighty roar, an enormous Pyrovile stepped out of the cave, lowering its head to fit. Lucius stared up in awe. It was one thing to catch glimpses of a face in billowing steam, but it was quite another to see an actual god in front of you, right there. They were really here. Everything he had done for them was justified. All the scores of people he had walked over, exiled and entombed, all were in service of this moment. He was sure they would have seen it that way, if they were still alive.

The Pyrovile beckoned to Lucius and the others. Lucius marched forward, without hesitation. The soldiers looked terrified, and didn't move. Lucius turned to glare at them. 'You have your orders. You would disobey the gods themselves?'

Lucius kept going. The soldiers scuttled in after him, carrying the marble squares.

Dawn was breaking. Caecilius and Metella blew out the candles, preparing the atrium for the day. They looked out of the window. In the distance, Vesuvius rumbled and smoked constantly.

'Sunrise, my love,' said Caecilius, trying to make the best of things despite his concerns. 'A new day! Even the longest night must end.'

'The mountain's worse than ever,' said Metella, worried. The dead Pyrovile had been cleared away, but the broken hypocaust was an ominous reminder of what had happened the night before. 'We killed a messenger of the gods in our own house. There'll be consequences.'

Caecilius shook his head. He was having none of it. 'If they were happy to let our daughter slowly turn to stone and to murder poor Rhombus, then I don't particularly care what they say. I'm starting to think it was purely Lucius and the Sisterhood rather than anything heavenly. Surely the gods wouldn't be so cruel when we've only ever done what they told us.'

'That's what I'm worried about,' said Metella. 'The gods can be vengeful, but only with good reason. People rarely need an excuse to do others ill.'

Caecilius nodded, gravely. Some of the cruellest acts in recent history had been committed by ordinary people, claiming to be in service of a higher power. The local vigilantes dispensed ever more cruel punishments, partly to deter future criminals, but mainly for their own amusement. They always claimed that the gods demanded it, without any proof. It hadn't shaken Caecilius's faith in the gods, but he definitely didn't trust anyone as much as he used to. Right now, Lucius and his cohorts were at the very bottom of the list of trustworthy people. There would be difficult days ahead, no doubt. But at least the family had each other.

Evelina walked in with Quintus. She still looked tired and drawn, but slightly more engaged with the world about her.

'Sweetheart, are you feeling better?' asked Metella. 'What can you see? What's going to happen?'

'Just leave her alone,' said Quintus. 'She's not one of them any more, she just wants to be normal.'

'It's all right. I can still see,' said Evelina. 'I can see . . .' She closed her eyes, and frowned. Something bad was coming. Very soon, very bad, and very close.

She turned her head quickly, as if trying to avoid the oncoming day. Her eyes sprang back open, and she drew a sharp intake of breath.

'What is it?' said Metella.

'A choice,' said Evelina, looking haunted, tears welling up. 'Someone must make the most terrible choice.'

Chapter XIII

Mea culpa

The Doctor and Donna ran deeper into the caverns inside Vesuvius. Donna hadn't given up trying to talk the Doctor round and, now that they had uncovered the Pyrovile interference, she was convinced that surely it was enough for him to step in. If not, she was more than prepared to step in herself, and put a stop to things.

'So, it's aliens,' she said, scrambling to keep up with him. 'Aliens are mucking about with the volcano, turning people to stone, doing all sorts. We know that, now. Doesn't that make it all right for you to stop it?'

'No,' said the Doctor, looking annoyed that they were still having this argument.

'But that's what you do, you stop bad people doing bad things. This lot are Very Bad People, and they're about to do a Very Bad Thing. You've got to stop them.'

'It's still part of history.'

Donna just couldn't wrap her head around it. How could he be so sure? 'But ... *I'm* history to you, technically. You saved me back when we first met, you've been hanging around in the future, way before you ever knew me. Don't I count as history too? You saved me, though, saved us all. How is that different?'

'Some things are just fixed, some things are in flux. Pompeii is fixed.'

'How do you know? How do you know which is which?'

The Doctor stopped to catch his breath, frustrated. 'Because that's how I see the universe! Every waking second. What is, what was, would could be, what must not be. That's the burden of a Time Lord, Donna. And I'm the only one left.'

Most of the time, the Doctor looked like a regular human being, even though Donna knew he wasn't. But sometimes, the mask slipped, and she could see the alien that he really was, as clearly as if he was a giant insect or something. She could see it now. He wasn't human. Nowhere near. He wasn't of this planet, at all. It was too easy to forget that, sometimes.

'How many people died here?' asked Donna, quietly. He might be an alien, but he still had a heart. Two hearts, in fact.

'Stop it.'

'Doctor. How many died?'

'About 20,000.'

'And when you see the universe, do you see them?

Can you see all 20,000 of them? Do you think that's all right? Don't you care about them?'

'Of course I care!' he said, angrily. 'You think I enjoy letting people die?'

'No, but—'

'Suppose I break all the rules and stop this. What then? Where does it end, Donna? Do I stop every disaster that ever happened? On every planet? Stop every murder in history? Accidents? How about people having bad thoughts who are about to do something, do I stop them before they do it? What would that make me? I don't want to be a dictator. I just do what I can, where I can, but when it's a fixed point in history, there's nothing I can do. And sometimes, yes, that means watching people die. Sometimes people I love.'

The Doctor turned away, annoyed at himself. His vulnerable side was showing, and now he briefly looked human again. Maybe Donna was rubbing off on him. After all, she couldn't have been *more* human, the humanity was practically pouring out of her.

'I know you care,' said Donna gently. 'I know it's difficult, what you do, but I just want to save these people. You have to understand that.'

'I want to save them too. But that's the catch, doing this all the time. You can't save everyone. It takes a toll.'

'Well then, don't take the burden all on yourself.'

'I have to.'

'No, you don't,' said Donna. 'I'm your friend. You know what they say – a problem shared, is . . . well, it's still a problem, but at least someone else gets to be miserable about it with you.'

The Doctor couldn't help smiling. 'Yeah,' he nodded.

'So let's go and do what we can, whatever that is,' said Donna. She punched his shoulder in a friendly way, trying to show solidarity, but slightly overdid it, making him wince.

'Ow,' he said. 'I don't think you know your own strength sometimes.'

'Sorry, yeah. Handy when things kick off down the local, though. Even if Sandra from Accounts started it and you were just innocently sitting in the corner, but as usual, I'm the one that gets blamed—'

They both jumped, as the loud foghorn rumble started up again. Now they were in the tunnels, it was incredibly loud, echoing through the caverns and pockets of rock. They covered their ears, but it didn't make much difference.

The sound gradually died away.

'Harmonic tremors,' said the Doctor. 'Magma pushing against solid rock. Wasn't supposed to happen here like this, but then neither was the rain of birds. And the frequency of the sound is different to the last time. Only slightly, but definitely higher than before. That's odd.'

Donna raised an eyebrow. '*That's* odd? Being a

different frequency is odd, but you being able to hear what frequency it is, that's perfectly normal, yeah?'

'I'm a Time Lord. I can hear all sorts of things. My ears are bigger on the inside.'

Donna rolled her eyes. 'Course they are.'

'It's getting more unstable in here,' said the Doctor. 'Let's keep moving.'

'Yes, good thinking, let's go further into the unstable volcano, what could possibly go wrong . . .'

'Come on, where's your sense of adventure?'

Donna snorted. 'It's running away, very fast, in the opposite direction. And I think it might have wet itself a bit. This feels a bit like tempting fate.'

The WHUMP of giant footsteps sounded again. The entire tunnel shook, small rocks and dust sifting down from above. It got closer.

'Another foot soldier,' said the Doctor. 'It's following us. They know we're here. They've got the psychic link. She must have told them to look for us.'

The whumping got closer. Louder.

'Run?' suggested Donna.

'Run,' agreed the Doctor.

They hurried through another tunnel, finding a dead end. The Doctor backed up and came to a fork in the path. He hesitated.

'Don't tell me we're lost,' said Donna.

'Well it's not like I can stop and ask for directions!' the Doctor protested.

They turned a corner, and saw an open area up ahead. The Doctor snapped his fingers and pointed, grinning. 'Ah! There we are, see, not lost, I knew exactly where I was going the whole time,' he said.

They cautiously snuck into the huge cavern, which contained several huge Pyrovile, all overseeing some sort of construction operation. Pits were dug in several areas, with cables sunk into each one. At the centre of it all was a large rock sphere about the size of a minibus, with all the pit cables leading into the open door. The cavern looked like a building site but, instead of diggers and cranes, there were giant magma creatures made of rock and flame stomping around.

The Doctor and Donna stayed hidden behind a rock formation, watching the activity.

'It's the heart of Vesuvius,' said the Doctor. 'We're right inside the volcano.'

'Shouldn't we have melted by now?' asked Donna. 'I mean, I'm not complaining, but . . .'

'No, you're right. The heat in here is much lower than it should be. I'm guessing it's something to do with whatever that is.'

He pointed at the rock sphere, then pulled out a mini telescope to get a closer look at it. Behind them, the heavy footsteps were still approaching.

'You'd better hurry up and think of something,' said Donna. 'Rocky 4's on his way.'

'Maybe that's how they arrived,' said the Doctor,

examining the rock sphere, trying to piece it all together. 'Or what's left of it. Escape pod? Prison ship? Gene bank?'

'But why do they need a volcano? Maybe it erupts, and they use it to launch themselves back into space or something?'

'Oh, I think it's worse than that.'

'How could it be worse?'

'I think they want the whole planet,' said the Doctor.

Donna sighed. 'I should have known not to ask, with you it can *always* be worse,' she said. But then a thought struck her. 'Wait, wait, wait! If they're the ones making the volcano erupt, that's alien intervention, right? Not a natural disaster? They're changing history, not you. Maybe Pompeii is a fixed point in time, but not because of the eruption, maybe it's because there isn't supposed to be one. You'd just be putting things back the way they're meant to be. That's what you do! You stop people breaking history. Maybe this bit of history has always been broken?'

'Maybe,' said the Doctor, thinking it through. It made sense. 'It's so ingrained into the culture, I never questioned it. Maybe that's why it's a fixed point, maybe it's supposed to be a fixed point when things are put back to rights. That's why they kept the circuit boards secret: they're not supposed to be here at all, and didn't want anyone like me stumbling across them.'

Donna was excited. There was a chance. A slim chance. 'So can we stop them?'

The Doctor nodded, tentatively at first, then more firmly. 'If I can, then yes. I will stop them. I will stop them *cold*.'

'Come on, then,' said Donna, itching to get stuck in. 'Let's go and interfere.'

'Right,' said the Doctor. 'Here's the plan. They haven't seen us down there yet, so the crucial advantage we have right now is the element of surprise. Which means—'

'Heathens!' cried Lucius, who had spotted them. He was standing on a higher ridge, pointing at them.

'You were saying, about the element of surprise?' said Donna.

'Yeah, that's blown that, I suppose,' said the Doctor.

'Defilers!' continued Lucius. 'They would desecrate your temple, my Lord Gods!'

Several Pyrovile turned to look.

'Rumbled,' muttered Donna.

The Doctor grabbed her hand, and pulled her forward, towards the rock sphere. 'Come on!'

'We can't go down there,' said Donna, alarmed. 'We don't even know what that thing is.'

'Well, we can't go back,' said the Doctor.

Lucius was still shouting, getting carried away. 'Crush them! Burn them!'

The Doctor and Donna raced towards the centre of the cavern. A Pyrovile stood in their way for a moment, until the Doctor squirted his water pistol at it. The tiny jets of water stung it enough to make it flinch, giving them a moment's respite to dodge it and run past. The creature looked at the tiny sizzles of water on its arm, puzzled at the mild effect of the weapon.

'Do we have a strategy for this?' asked Donna. 'Or are we just hoping for random inspiration?'

'Little bit from Column A, little bit from Column B,' said the Doctor.

'This is not the time to be winging it!'

'Thinking, thinking!' said the Doctor. 'Hey, at least they don't have weapons.'

Another Pyrovile reared up near them, and made a sword of fire appear in its hand, extending its internal flames out to create a large, burning blade.

'Stop saying things!' said Donna. 'You keep saying things won't happen, and then they happen! Stop it!'

'Sorry!' said the Doctor. 'Can't help it. Hey, at least we're not—'

'Ahhhh! Stop saying things!'

They reached the rock sphere, but were now surrounded by Pyrovile. Lucius looked down at them, triumphant.

'There is nowhere to run, Doctor, and Daughter of London,' he sneered.

The Doctor held his hands out, conceding. 'Now

then, Lucius,' he said. 'And my Lords Pyrovillian. Don't get yourself in a lava. In a *lava*! No?'

The joke fell flat. Even Donna shook her head, disappointed. 'No,' she said.

'No,' said the Doctor. Oh well. 'But if I might beg the wisdom of the gods before we perish? Your chance to gloat, you clearly love the sound of your own voice. Feel free to tell us how beaten we are, how we have been utterly defeated. Once this new race of creatures is complete, then what?'

Lucius looked smug, and started grandstanding. 'My masters will follow the example of Rome itself. An almighty empire, bestriding the whole of civilisation.'

'Or,' said Donna, 'and hear me out – you could go home. You crashed here, but you've got all this technology now. Why not just go?'

'The Heaven of Pyrovillia is gone,' said Lucius.

'What do you mean, gone?' asked the Doctor. 'Where's it gone?'

'It is lost, a world stolen from the firmament.'

'Mucked about with one volcano too many, did they?' said Donna.

'The Heaven of Pyrovillia is gone,' Lucius intoned again. 'But there is heat enough in this world for a new species to rise.'

'Yeah,' said the Doctor. 'I should warn you, it's 70 per cent water out there. Why is it the aliens who can't survive here who always turn up? You can even see the water from space, not like it's a surprise or anything.'

'Water can boil,' said Lucius. 'And everything will burn, Doctor.'

'That's what the converter was for,' the Doctor realised. It was all clear now. 'They're going to make the Earth habitable for them, which leaves it uninhabitable for human life. So! The whole planet is at stake. Thank you, that's all I needed to know. Donna!'

The Doctor grabbed Donna's arm and they ran into the rock sphere. He whipped out the sonic, and closed the door, locking them inside.

'You have them, my Lords!' shouted Lucius. A Pyrovile stomped over, and started breathing fire onto the sphere, trying to open it.

Inside the sphere, the Doctor and Donna crowded into the small chamber. The six marble squares were now embedded into the wall, forming a full circuit board. They hummed and glowed as the electronic signals pulsed through them. Whatever Lucius had been constructing, this was it, and it was working. The Doctor examined the squares and connections, quickly trying to get a sense of how it all worked.

Donna looked around the cramped space. 'Could we be any more trapped?' she said. They didn't seem to be in a better position in here, now they had nowhere to go.

The sound of the fire outside got louder, and the

temperature began to rise. Donna tried not to panic. 'Bit hot,' she said.

The Doctor checked the controls, hitting buttons, and examining the results. He waved his hands around wildly, explaining how it all worked, barely able to keep up with himself as he spoke, practically tripping over the words. 'See?' he said. 'The energy converter takes the lava, uses the power from the heat to create a fusion matrix, which welds Pyrovile to human. Now it's complete, they can convert millions. Turn the Earth into a volcano planet. You think it's hot in here, wait until they're finished with everything out there.'

The Doctor stopped. He had realised something. This was very bad.

'But can't you fix it with these controls?' said Donna, oblivious to his sudden change in demeanour.

'Of course I can, but don't you see? That's why the Soothsayers can't see the volcano. There *is* no volcano! Vesuvius is never going to erupt. The Pyrovile are stealing all its power. They're going to use it to take over the world.'

'OK, but you just said you could change it back.'

'Yes. I can invert the system, then all that energy and heat will flow back into the heart of the volcano, putting everything back to normal.'

Donna's face lit up. 'That's brilliant! So you can fix it after all, you can stop what they're trying to do. Let's do it, then!'

The Doctor looked haggard. He shook his head. 'Back to normal, meaning, the volcano will erupt. The Pyrovile will be destroyed, the Earth will be saved. But the eruption will happen. That's the choice, Donna. It's Pompeii or the world.'

Donna stared at him, as the weight of it sank in. He was right. It was worse. Much, much worse. 'Oh, my God,' she breathed.

The Doctor looked resigned to it, almost as if he had expected something bad like this to happen. 'If Pompeii is destroyed, then it's not just history. It's *me*. I make it happen.'

'Maybe there's another way,' said Donna. 'The Pyrovile are made of rocks, maybe they can't be blown up by an eruption, maybe we have to think of something else—'

'Donna,' said the Doctor, gently. 'It's the only way to stop them. Vesuvius explodes with the force of two dozen nuclear bombs. Nothing can survive it. Not the Pyrovile. Certainly not us.'

Donna knew it had to be done. She hated to admit it, especially when they'd only just started their adventures together. But if this really was the end, then at least they'd go out on a high, literally saving the world. Very few people would get to do that. 'Never mind us,' she said, ever so quietly.

The Doctor nodded, and they shared a silent moment together, both of them knowing what needed to be done. He pressed some more buttons, adjusted a few others, and then pointed at a lever.

'Push this lever, and it's over.'

He reached for the lever, and hesitated. Such a simple thing, pushing a lever. Simple, but with such a profoundly terrible outcome. The decision came so easily to many of the villains he'd come up against, they didn't even stop to think about the deaths they caused. He would never, *could* never understand that.

He carefully put his hands on the lever, without pressing it. The chamber was getting hotter and hotter as the Pyrovile outside blew flame onto the outside of the rock sphere. Soon, they would break through the shielding, and it would be too late to stop them. But the Doctor just couldn't bring himself to do it. 'Twenty thousand people,' he said, distraught.

Donna saw the anguish in his face. There was no way to avoid it, nobody had a better option here, but what a terrible burden, knowing that you were going to be responsible for so many deaths. Even if it was to save so many more.

It was the sort of burden nobody should ever have to face alone. A burden that should be shared.

By a friend.

Donna placed her hands over the Doctor's on the lever. If it had to be done, then they'd do it together. They would both have to live with it. Of course, it would still hurt, but they'd always know that the other understood how it felt.

They looked at each other. The Doctor, still upset, but so grateful to have Donna there in that moment. Donna, sick with fear over what they were about to do, but determined not to let him do it alone. An unspoken bond between them.

It was time.

Together, they pushed the lever.

Chapter XIV

Memento mori

And in Pompeii, the world ended.

Chapter XV

Tenebrae

As soon as the lever went down, Evelina threw her head back, rocked by a vision. An awful, new vision. Something that would linger for the rest of her life, burned into her memory.

The images appeared in her mind, unbidden. Horrible scenes of the mountain exploding, killing every man, woman and child in Pompeii. Including her family. She saw them crushed beneath tons of rocks and dust, unable to breathe, their final moments spent in unbearable pain and fear. A sad, lonely end.

She couldn't tell them. They didn't need to know, and telling them wouldn't make a difference, there was no escape from it. She didn't even want to think about it, but had no choice, the ugly images were right there in her head, clear as day, even if she closed her eyes.

Tears fell down Evelina's face. 'The future . . . is changing . . .' she said.

*

In the Temple, all of the other Sisters were hit by the same horrendous vision. Everyone who had been given the gift of sight saw the same thing. It hit them like a falling slab of marble, and seemed to weigh just as much.

'A new prophecy,' gasped Spurrina, dropping to all fours as her legs weakened. How could she not have seen this? They always saw everything, they were never wrong. It was so huge, how was this hidden from them? Was it deliberate? Why?

Spurrina looked over at the High Priestess, who screeched in pain, collapsing, the sheer weight of the vision pulling her to the ground.

It was all over. Everything they had worked for was about to be undone, and there was nothing they could do about it. After all this time, their story was finally over.

When the Doctor had reversed the energy converter, it sent all the heat and power flowing right back into Vesuvius. It was a volcano once more. Immediately, the magma churned, turning the cavern from a construction site into an inferno. Molten rock spewed in fountains as the ground collapsed, and fire rained from the ceiling.

'No!' screamed Lucius, in the heart of Vesuvius, as the same vision burst into his mind. 'My Lords were supposed to inherit this world!' Once again, Lucius had been let down by those he put his trust in. They were exposed as the liars and manipulators that they really were. And he had helped them to do all of it. At least they would suffer the same fate as him, although it was small consolation. He howled at the injustice of it all. No one heard. No one cared.

A sheet of flame from the mountain silenced him for ever.

With an ear-shattering crack, the volcano erupted. Effortlessly, it sent a massive chunk of the mountain-top into the air, as if it was weightless. The cloud spread out impossibly fast.

Rock vomited up, almost immediately fragmenting into billions of particles of dust and rock. A waterfall in reverse, with stone instead of water. The gushing roar echoed far and wide across the country.

A mile-high column of smoke, ash and rock was thrust upwards at over 300 miles per hour, seemingly puncturing the sky. It blocked out the sunlight, turning day to night. The volcano forced out, on average, 10,000 tons of debris *every second*. At its peak, the eruption cloud would reach a height of 20 miles. Already, it was raining ash and debris on Pompeii.

But that was merely the start of it.

In the midst of the eruption, the rock sphere hurtled up into the sky. The Doctor and Donna were thrown around inside.

'Are we dead?' yelled Donna, huddled against one wall.

The Doctor checked the controls. 'No, this must have been an old escape pod that survived the crash, the only part of their ship they had left.' He used the sonic to activate some of the buttons. 'There, inertial dampeners! Just about still working, otherwise we'd have been crushed against the walls—'

'How have we not melted?'

'They converted the pod housing to use the heat from the volcano. Now I'm using it to stop us from burning up. We might just get out of this in one piece. Hang on!'

Everything shook as the sphere hit the ground, bouncing back up before falling back down again. The Doctor and Donna tumbled around inside as if they were in a washing machine, the pod eventually banging and clattering to a halt at the foot of a hillside, miles outside Pompeii.

The door fell open, and they tumbled out, battered and bruised, but alive.

The Doctor looked back at the eruption. It looked like they had landed in a battlefield, smoke and flames everywhere, red hot chunks of flaming rock landing all around them. It was a warzone, but the only victor was the mountain.

Eyeing the vengeful sky, the Doctor and Donna

started running back towards Pompeii. They had to reach the TARDIS. There was no time to waste now.

In the villa, Caecilius looked out of the window, while Metella and Quintus comforted Evelina, who was still in the grip of the psychic images. Caecilius watched as the enormous smoke plume blotted out the sun, and stared in horror as ash and chunks of rock started raining down in the streets.

'The heavens are falling,' he whispered, unable to comprehend what was happening in any other terms.

Evelina's eyelids fluttered, as the last remaining fragments of the vision faded away from her mind. Heartbroken, she knew they would never leave this room again.

'Death,' she said. 'Only death.'

Out on the streets, traffic and trade had ground to a halt. Everyone was staring at the smoke, flinching at the noise. Some of them uselessly brushed ash from their clothes, while others ran away, starting to panic. They still had no idea what had actually happened. The mountain had always rumbled and smoked and shaken the ground, but it had never done anything like this, on this scale.

The ash and rock built up fast, shockingly fast. Within minutes, the roofs on small buildings were starting to collapse. Even then, nobody knew it meant the end of Pompeii. They had no way to fully understand what they were seeing.

The cloud grew, until there was no trace of sun any more.

Night had fallen, in the afternoon.

Quickly, unstoppably, the debris began to bury the city.

In the Temple of Sibyl, part of the roof had collapsed. Most of the Sisters had fled, gone to where they thought they would be safe, elsewhere in the city. But nowhere was safe.

Spurrina cradled Mira the Soothsayer, whose head had been gashed by a chunk of falling rock. Nearby, the High Priestess was dying, the light from the flames within her growing dim and faint now that the source of her power had been taken away. She was the very last of her kind left, and she knew it, she felt the pain of the others as they were destroyed. Spurrina looked over at her, without pity.

'You lied to us,' she said. But despite the deception, she knew that somehow, impossibly, this was meant to be. 'This was always supposed to happen,' she whispered to Mira.

Mira nodded faintly.

Spurrina didn't know how they hadn't seen it before. But things had been put right now.

For what it was worth.

It took the Doctor and Donna several hours to get back. The ground was treacherous, and the rain of debris was more solid now, much more dangerous than the initial shower. Fist-sized burning rocks were slamming down everywhere, making small craters in the ground.

'Come on,' said the Doctor, urgently. 'We have to reach the TARDIS before everything gets buried.'

'And the people?' said Donna.

The Doctor didn't answer.

When they reached the city, it was chaos. The ash and small rocks were a constant rain, and the larger chunks were smashing through buildings and people. Panic had well and truly set in. Nobody knew what to do or where to go. Some just ran in circles, terrified, screaming, unable to decide which direction to go. There was no escaping the sky.

The ground was misshapen, lumpy from the build-up of ash and rock. The Doctor and Donna stumbled along on the top layer, making slow progress.

A group of people ran down the street, heading towards the beach. Donna held her hands up, attempting to stop them. She was in tears.

'No! Wait!' she shouted, trying to warn them. 'Don't go to the beach! Go to the hills, you'll be safer up there!

Please! Don't go to the beach, it won't protect you! Listen to me!'

Wild-eyed, they just pushed her away, running around her. They were in a state of total panic and, even if they could hear her over the noise, they had no reason to believe her. The Doctor let her try for a while, knowing that he couldn't talk her out of it. He had to give her this much, if nothing else.

Donna saw a lone child, lost, crying in a corner. She picked him up, but the child's mother came running over, frantic, grabbing him back off her, thinking some crazed stranger was stealing her son.

'Wait! Please! You can't go that way!' warned Donna. But it was no use. The mother ran off with her child, into the smoke and darkness. Towards the shore.

'Come on,' said the Doctor.

'They all got killed on the beach,' said Donna. 'We learned about it at school. They told us what happened to them, it was so horrible, and the ones in Herculaneum, they were boiled by the hot air, Doctor they were just *boiled*—'

'There's nothing you can do. You can't save them. You know that.'

'But there must be something . . .' Donna whirled around, her face streaked with ash and tears. Utterly distraught. So many people running to their own doom. They didn't know it, but they were going to their own graves, where they would remain, entombed and undiscovered, for centuries.

'Donna,' said the Doctor, as gently as he could. 'That giant cloud is going to collapse at any minute, and send a huge pyroclastic surge across this entire city. A cloud of ash and gas, three times the heat of boiling water. We won't survive that. We have to go. You know we do.'

The Doctor kept moving, and Donna had no choice but to follow, throwing a last, agonised glance back over her shoulder.

Much, much later, Donna would continue to be haunted by the memory of that child. Sometimes, late at night, trying to get to sleep, she would see his tear-streaked face.

Chapter XVI

Deus ex machina

Caecilius had managed to seal the compluvium opening above the atrium, and so far it had kept out the worst of the ash and rocks. Dust drifted down as more and more debris settled on the roof. The beams buckled and creaked alarmingly. It looked like it was snowing indoors, there was so much ash falling.

He and his family huddled together in the corner, with a few of their valuables thrown to one side next to them. They had hoped to make a run for it, but it just wasn't safe. Besides, they had no idea where to go. Nobody did.

He glanced up at the roof, nervously, as it creaked some more. More dust sifted through the cracks.

'What is it?' asked Metella.

'Just wondering how much more the roof can take,' said Caecilius. 'Most of the others in the street have collapsed already.'

'It'll hold,' said Quintus. 'You built it to be strong.

We'll be fine. My dad is the best architect in all the land.'

'That's right,' joined in Evelina. 'I bet when this is all over, ours will be the only house left standing.'

Caecilius looked at them gratefully. All his regrets played out on his face, in quick succession. 'I'm sorry we never moved to Rome,' he said. 'You all wanted to, but no, I had to stay here, be a big fish in a small pond. So stupid.'

'Stop that now,' said Metella, firmly. 'Don't be silly. We don't care where we live, or . . . as long as the family is together. I wouldn't want to be anywhere else.'

'Me neither,' said Evelina.

'Hey, I go where the wine is,' said Quintus, smiling.

Tears brimming, Caecilius hugged them all.

They sat in the corner, waiting for the end, wondering how much more terror they could realistically feel before going numb.

A commotion outside made them look up. Their strange visitors, the Doctor and Donna, had forced their way in through the front door, and were running towards the blue box. They stopped when they saw the family. Odd, thought Caecilius. They almost looked guilty, but he couldn't imagine why.

'Gods save us, Doctor,' said Caecilius, trying to put on a brave face. 'You're welcome to stay here and take shelter.'

The Doctor couldn't even look at them.

'Is it the end of the world?' asked Evelina.

Finally, the Doctor met their eyes. Looking haunted.

'No,' he said. 'It's not.'

The words should have held some comfort, but for some reason, they had the opposite effect. If he hadn't been sweating in the heat, Caecilius thought he might have been chilled to the bone.

The Doctor dashed to the blue box, and unexpectedly opened a door in the side of it, running inside. Caecilius didn't know it could do that, or why they wanted to go in there. Maybe they thought they'd be safer inside it, if the roof of the villa collapsed.

'No!' shouted Donna. 'Doctor, you can't. Doctor!'

She followed him, looking back at the family, guilt-stricken.

'It was nice to meet you both,' said Caecilius.

Donna smiled sadly at him, and seemed as if she was looking at a ghost. She disappeared inside, the door closed, and a strange, wheezing, grinding sound filled the air. Bizarrely, impossibly, the blue box started fading away, until it disappeared entirely. Caecilius blinked the ash out of his eyes, confused. Did he really see that? Was he suffering from heat exhaustion? No time to worry about it right now. Not much time for anything at all.

He kept his arms around his family, pulling them closer.

*

Inside the TARDIS, the Cloister Bell was tolling its deep, ominous chime. The Doctor had already started the engines. Donna marched in.

'You can't just leave them,' she said. She felt drained by the past couple of days, but she had just enough fuel left in the tank to fight him on this.

'Don't you think I've done enough?' said the Doctor, slamming controls and hitting buttons. 'History's back in place, and everyone dies.'

'You've got to go back. Doctor, I am telling you, take this thing BACK. It's not fair!' She was openly crying now, tears pouring down her face. Angry at herself for letting the tears fall, but if you couldn't cry for these people, who could you cry for?

'No, it's not fair,' said the Doctor. 'The universe isn't fair.'

There he was, thought Donna. There was the alien. She could see him now, truly, openly. He wasn't cold, or callous, just . . . *other*. He'd picked up a lot of human traits, over a long time, he could easily pass for someone from Earth. He was genuinely kind, warm, funny, sweet. But there was more to him. A lot more. Not all of it good. Donna was incapable of fully understanding how he saw the universe, just as much as he could never quite see it how she did. If she had his knowledge, his power, his technology, she would be physically incapable of *not* trying to save everyone. She probably wouldn't get very far, and doubted that she'd have had as many adventures as him, she'd have started way too many fights and things would undoubtedly have gone very wrong early on. But she'd have given her last breath to at least try. Why couldn't she get through to him? She tried again.

'But your own planet! It burned.'

'That's just it. Don't you see, Donna? Can't you understand? If I could go back and save them, then I would. But I can't. I can never go back. I just can't.'

The TARDIS lurched as the Doctor kept slamming controls. He wasn't angry at her, Donna realised. He was angry at himself, for not being able to fix everything. And in that moment, her fury trickled away completely. She understood him a tiny bit better. But they still had to do something.

'Just someone,' she said, quietly, still crying softly. 'Please. Not the whole town. Just save *someone*.'

The Doctor stared at her, across the console, for a long, long time.

Donna had no idea what would happen next, if anything. But she was spent. She'd pleaded with all of her energy.

Still staring at her, the Doctor slammed down a lever.

Back in the villa, the roof had almost completely buckled inwards. Rubble and ash fell heavily through the cracks. The ash 'snowfall' was drifting in the corners of the room, and flames were starting to lick at the doors as the air outside became superheated.

It was nearly the end.

In the corner, the family were all covered in a layer of dust now. Caecilius kept his arms tightly around them, desperately trying to keep them safe despite the overwhelming threat, as if his arms could somehow hold back the forces of nature. He knew it was futile, but it was instinct. He didn't know what else to do.

Another, bigger beam cracked, incredibly loudly, making them all scream.

A louder noise started to fill the villa, a low rumble, a grinding, wheezing sound. Was this the end? Were the roof and walls finally giving up to the huge pressure outside?

A light shone, getting brighter.

The sound became more familiar. They had heard it just a few minutes before.

The family looked up, in awe, as the strange blue box started to reappear out of nowhere, right in front of them this time. The light on top shone out in the darkness.

Finally, it became fully solid, somehow having moved itself across the room.

The door opened, and light blazed out from inside. The family squinted as the light hit their eyes. The Doctor stood there, in the doorway, and held his hand out.

'Come with me,' he said.

Caecilius wasn't sure how they would all fit into the box, but maybe it would be an extra layer of shelter when the villa finally collapsed. He reached out, took the Doctor's hand, and led the family forwards, in through the door.

The door closed behind them, and they stopped, staring in shock.

They were in a vast chamber, seemingly made of stone and light. In the centre, some kind of large table glittered and sparkled, as a column rose up and down, the source of the strange grinding noise.

The Doctor ran to the table, and started moving things around. Donna was there, smiling at them happily, wiping tears from her face. She beckoned them further in, but they stayed by the door, too scared to move. This place was too big, too bright, too *wrong*. Caecilius worried that if they moved too far from the doorway, they'd be lost for ever in this strange, cavernous place. He didn't understand what was happening.

'This place,' whispered Evelina. 'The inside is the wrong size. It's the wrong way round.'

The others were too frightened to speak. They stayed huddled together.

Almost immediately, it was over, and the grinding sounds slowed to a stop. The Doctor and Donna came over and opened the door. Caecilius flinched – why were they going back into the villa? Surely they were safer in here, bizarre though it was?

But when he looked out of the door, they were no longer in the villa. The box had moved once again.

He led the family outside, hesitantly. They were up on a hill, quite far from Pompeii, able to overlook the devastation safely. How was this possible, so quickly? He didn't want to question it, in case the reality was fragile enough to shatter under scrutiny. What mattered was that somehow, they were all safe.

The rest of Pompeii wasn't so lucky. Caecilius wondered how they were doing in Herculaneum, which was even closer to the mountain. He didn't know that the city and people there no longer existed.

The enormous cloud over Vesuvius had collapsed, and the pyroclastic flow surged forward, covering the entirety of Pompeii in a blanket of ash and rocks. This was the third pyroclastic surge, and the first one to reach Pompeii. There would be six surges in all, but the damage was already done.

Their beautiful city was completely buried.

The family watched in silence, upset to see their home vanish before their eyes. But they were together. Safe. Alive.

The Doctor and Donna stood next to them. No matter who they were, no matter how powerful, they obviously weren't immune to this terrible sight. That was some consolation. The Doctor seemed to guess what Caecilius was thinking, and put a hand on his shoulder.

'It's never forgotten,' said the Doctor. 'Oh, time will pass, people will move on, and stories will fade. But one day, Pompeii will be found again. Years from now, it will become a monument to what happened, to the people who lived here. And everyone will remember you.'

The Doctor didn't have the visions, the sight, but Caecilius somehow knew he was telling the truth. As if he had already seen it, already been there, in the future.

'Thank you, so much,' said Caecilius. 'You saved us. You saved our family.'

'What about you, Evelina?' asked Donna. 'Can you see anything?'

'The visions have gone,' said Evelina, sounding relieved. She didn't want anything to do with what had happened, and never again wanted to know anything in advance. She already looked healthier, even her arm was starting to heal.

The Doctor nodded. 'The explosion was so power-ful, it cracked open a rift in time, just for a second,' he said. 'That's what gave you all the gift of prophecy. It echoed back into the Pyrovillian alternative. But not any more. You're free.'

Caecilius wasn't sure what most of that meant, but it sounded reassuring, so he just nodded, gratefully. He was happy to take him at his word.

'But tell me,' said Metella, almost too afraid to ask.

161

'Who are you, Doctor? With your words, and your temple containing such size within?'

'Oh, I was never here,' winked the Doctor. 'Don't tell anyone.'

Caecilius stared at the clouds that still blotted out the sun. Lightning flashed inside them as they roiled and churned.

'The great god Vulcan must be enraged,' he said. 'It's so Vulcanic. Like some sort of . . .' And then he finally realised the meaning of the word the Doctor and Donna had used when they first met. 'Volcano,' he said. It made sense now, but was no comfort at all. The shock of it all hit him again, coming in waves. 'All those people,' he said, his legs buckling slightly.

Metella put her arm around him, holding him tightly. 'I know,' she said. They were going to get through this. The worst was over now. She repeated his words back to him. 'Even the longest night must end, my love.'

As the devastation slowed, Caecilius turned to thank their strange rescuers.

But they were gone, along with their box.

Chapter XVII

Status quo

The Doctor strolled around the console, absentmindedly operating switches and levers. He had calmed down now, as if a weight had been lifted.

Donna didn't know quite what to say. She was incredibly glad that the family was safe, distraught at the huge loss of life, relieved that the alien threat had been stopped, guilty at their involvement in the whole thing. It was an overwhelming mix of emotions. In the end, there was really only one thing to say.

'Thank you,' she said.

The Doctor nodded. Then stopped, reflecting on what had just happened. 'You were right, you know,' he said. 'Back when we first met. I didn't listen. Thought I knew better. But you were right. Sometimes I need someone.'

'Yeah,' said Donna.

'Besides, I didn't change much,' said the Doctor. 'A lot of people still died.'

'Not those four people. That matters.'

'I haven't done them any favours. They'll have no money, no belongings, they're homeless—'

'And alive!' interrupted Donna. 'They're alive. That's the most important thing. Take the win! They'll get back on their feet. Probably tell the story for generations. You made a difference. Isn't that why you do this?'

'People don't usually want to remember me. I only turn up when bad things happen.'

For a moment, this time, instead of the alien, Donna saw right into the Doctor's soul. The pain, the crushing pain, of all those he hadn't been able to save. The massive burden of being the last of his kind, trying to judge what to fix and what to leave well alone. It was only brief, barely a second or two, and then he abruptly closed the gap, bouncing back. Donna could see that he was papering over the sadness with forced jollity, but she let him get away with it, this time.

'Besides,' said the Doctor. 'I couldn't let someone die after they gave me a nice lunch. That would just be rude.'

'Yeah? What about the big, important Laws of Time? In the fancy book? The Laws of Time that can never be broken?'

'Oh, Laws of Time, Schmaws of Schmime. The Laws of Lunch overrule the Laws of Time. Anyway, don't think of it as throwing away the rulebook, more like tearing out half a page. I won't tell anyone if you don't.'

Donna mimed zipping her mouth shut, locking it, and throwing away the imaginary key.

'Blimey,' marvelled the Doctor, 'if I'd know it was that easy to get you to stop talking, I'd have done it ages ago.'

Her mouth still closed, Donna mumbled an angry comeback that was definitely stuffed with rude words.

'Don't worry,' said the Doctor. 'Sometimes I check in on people after I've left. Quietly, without letting them know. I'll keep an eye on the family for a bit. Make sure they're OK. Remind myself why I'm here, what I'm supposed to do. I'm not going to forget their faces in a hurry. Especially Caecilius, that's a good face. Strong face. I love a good face.'

Donna nodded, satisfied. It had been a long day, and she was exhausted. She'd run out of spoons for the day, as her friend Becca would say. A thought struck her. 'So, is that technically a "deus ex machina", then? You're basically godlike, or at least, godlike to them, this is your machine, so . . .'

'No. Nobody ever uses that phrase correctly. It means, a convenient ending where the solution comes out of nowhere, without being set up ahead of time. It doesn't just mean "an ending I didn't like", no matter what the internet says. So annoying.'

'All right, all right, excuse me Charles Dickens. Or was he an alien, too?'

'No, of course he wasn't, don't be silly.'

'That's a relief, at least.'

'Although . . . we did come across some aliens when we met, they were able to take over dead bodies and reanimate—'

'Never mind, sorry I asked, should have known better, my own fault.'

The Doctor ran around the console, getting ready for the next trip. 'Right. Let's go cause some trouble.'

He yanked a lever, purposefully, which immediately snapped off in his hand. Again.

'Ah, yes, I never did fix that,' he said. 'Still, shouldn't really be a prob—'

Everything lurched to one side, and something deep in the engines started clanking and crunching.

'Is that bad?' yelled Donna, over the din.

'Nah, don't worry, it's always doing that.'

'Right, that doesn't mean it's a good thing, though. Maybe we can stop off at a garage, along the way?'

'Hold tight! This might get a bit bumpy. And, er, crashy . . .'

The TARDIS whooshed through the time vortex, spinning wildly, off to the next adventure. Maybe it wouldn't be where – or when – the Doctor had planned to be. But it would always be exactly the place and time he *needed* to be.

Epilogue

Tabula rasa

Six months after the events in Pompeii, the family had resettled in Rome. In a way, they had rebuilt again, carrying on the traditions and memories of their home. They had to keep quiet about it, of course. They'd come up with a story about how they left Pompeii just before the eruption, and didn't mention any of the details. Besides, how else would they have explained it? The mountain exploded, but two people in a magic box flew them to safety? They weren't sure they believed it themselves, sometimes. It felt like a half-remembered dream, like none of it had really happened. Now and again, though, if there was a little thunder in the sky, or the crash of an overturned cart, it would trigger the memories, and it all came flooding back. The day that turned to night. The fear. The heat. Their strange rescuers.

It took a while to get back on their feet again, but they had a running start. Caecilius had been owed some marble from a quarry far outside the city, which was undamaged. They also discovered that somehow they had brought a large bag of their valuables with them. In the confusion, one of them must have grabbed it, but none of them could remember picking it up, or packing all of their stuff, or carrying it to Rome. It had simply turned up in their new home one day, like an afterthought. Just one of those things, they supposed.

They were able to use most of this to barter their way into the loan that got their business up and running. A few contracts later, along with some determination, a little luck, and a lot of hard work, they were making a nice living. Their new villa was a project Caecilius had taken on, refurbishing an abandoned building and making it beautiful once more. It was the pride of the street now, and quite the show house. They weren't as wealthy as before, but they were well on their way.

That day, Caecilius had a new contract meeting later in the morning. He fussed around as the family got themselves ready for the day. He searched the atrium frantically, trying to find everything he needed. Always a rush, always hustle and bustle, and that was just the way he liked it.

'Metella, my love,' he called out. 'Have you seen that clasp? The beetle one. The Egyptians do love a scarab.'

Metella walked over, an island of calm in the chaos. She handed him the clasp. 'Here we are. I was just giving it a polish. Now calm down!'

Caecilius fastened the clasp on, fingers fumbling in his haste. 'If I get that contract for the marble granaries of Alexandria, we'll be rich. You'll see.'

'Here, let me,' said Metella, fastening the clasp for him. 'Otherwise it'll take you all day, you'll be late, then you won't get the contract, and I shall be forced to throw you into the river and get myself a new husband. I'll be upset, of course, for several hours, maybe even days. But I'll do it.'

'It's as good as won,' smiled Caecilius. His smile vanished when he saw Evelina walk in wearing a short outfit. 'Hold on there, Evelina, you are not going out wearing that!'

Evelina rolled her eyes, a normal teenager now, which meant her parents were quite simply *the* most embarrassing people in the world. 'Don't start, Dad, it's what all the girls in Rome are wearing. See you later.'

She kissed him on the cheek, and ran out. Caecilius called after her. 'Are you seeing that boy again?' But she was already gone. 'I think she is, you know,' he said. 'I don't like him. His eyebrows are too high up on his face. Always looks surprised by everything.'

Quintus walked in, very well dressed, carrying some scrolls. Metella gasped in delight, as she admired his smart new look.

'Oh, look at Quintus!' she said. 'My son, the doctor!'

'Mum,' said Quintus, embarrassed but secretly proud. 'I've told you, I'm not a doctor. Not yet. I'm just a student of the physical sciences.'

'Well, that's a doctor to me,' said Metella, cupping his face, delighted. 'Give thanks to the Household Gods before you go, there's a good lad.' She saw Caecilius struggling to roll a sheet of parchment, and hurried over to him. 'Come here, let me fix it, you're doing it all wrong.'

Quintus walked over to an alcove, where the shrine to the Household Gods was. These days, he was happy to do it. In the past, he'd never quite believed he was talking to anyone real. But now he'd seen first-hand that they really were watching over them.

He dipped his hand in the wine, and sprinkled a few drops over the shrine.

'Thank you, Household Gods,' he said, full of sincerity. 'Thank you for everything.'

The shrine contained a new design, a hand-carved marble square. It was a bas-relief sculpture of two figures who looked very much like the Doctor and Donna, standing either side of a temple that looked a lot like the TARDIS. Carved into the TARDIS, instead of POLICE BOX, was PRAESIDIUM ARCA, which roughly translated as 'protection box'.

Quintus smiled at the figures. He stood, gathered his scrolls, and headed out.

*

Caecilius won the Egyptian contract, and the next few, too, becoming a hugely successful and respected architect. Things kept going the family's way, for quite some time. They didn't know if it was luck, or just the gods balancing things out after all the terrible things they'd been through before they got here.

Whatever it was, over time they continued to prosper and thrive. Quintus became a doctor, saving many lives. Evelina became a noted playwright, writing clever, popular tales that lifted people's spirits. Metella became a mediator between battling political rivals, gaining considerable influence and implementing security procedures at major summits.

They were all very talented at what they did, but when they started out, they all had several lucky breaks. A nudge here, a word there, the right time here, the right place there.

Almost as if someone was watching out for them.

They wouldn't know it yet, but their family held onto this luck for generations. Each new set of descendants was similarly fortunate, ensuring their continuing success. They were always drawn to the same sorts of careers – doctor, protector, architect, storyteller, variations on the theme, over and over again.

Thousands of years later, the latest incarnations of the family regularly joked that they must have a guardian angel watching over them.

They did. And they always will.

Acknowledgements

It takes a village to create anything. This book wouldn't exist without the script, which wouldn't exist without a ton of people, and I wouldn't have the script or a TV career without Russell T (for Television) Davies taking a chance on me. He is the kindest *and* toughest boss I've ever had, because he wants you to be your best and knows you can do it. I can never, ever thank him enough for everything he's done for me. So I won't. He doesn't need even *more* praise! I'll never hear the end of it!

Jason Arnopp was a constant cheerleader. When I was convinced I wouldn't be able to do a good job, he talked me down, built me up and politely asked me to please stop shrieking through his window at 3.33am every night. There are lots of words in this book, but this paragraph is just his.

Scott K Andrews very kindly read the first few chapters and reassured me that I was able to string a sentence together, and should carry on, which was a huge relief.

Steve Cole (editor) and Steve Tribe (copy-editor) were immensely patient with me, holding my hand through the entire process and removing thousands of extraneous commas, while gently explaining how books work and what 'grammar' is (apparently it's important, don't ask me, I have no idea).

Cat, my better half (and a much better writer than me), always keeps me honest and safe, and makes me braver than I ever thought I could be. Let's go conquer the universe together (in a nice way; no blowing up planets or anything, unless they're blocking the road).